The Last Great Gun

The governor had a vision – grant amnesty to the killers plaguing his territory, then enlist them to work for him in purging the land of the outlaw hordes.

He never expected Rogan, the wildest one of all, to apply. But when he did it was celebrated as proof that amnesty could work. But the young gunman had other ideas. He would accept amnesty and win the governor's confidence. Then shoot him down.

Could anything but a bullet stop him? Could such a man ever change?

The Last Great Gun

Clint Ryker

A Black Horse Western

ROBERT HALE · LONDON

© Clint Ryker 2007
First published in Great Britain 2007

ISBN 978-0-7090-8425-9

Robert Hale Limited
Clerkenwell House
Clerkenwell Green
London EC1R 0HT

www.halebooks.com

Typeset by
Derek Doyle & Associates, Shaw Heath
Printed and bound in Great Britain by
Antony Rowe Limited, Wiltshire

CHAPTER 1

ALWAYS THE GUNS

Nothing could be as dark as a starless Badlands midnight as the wind suddenly rose with an eerie whisper then shifted uncertainly over the Riata Creek camp, rustling in the trees and rippling the surface of dark waters of The Hole.

A single finger of wind dipped out of the blackness and lifted a gust of powdery ash from the fire and dusted it across the two motionless, blanket-shrouded shapes lying side-by-side upon the hard earth. It feathered the manes and tails of the sleeping horses before falling away to die, leaving the night hushed once more . . . yet not quite still.

The dull thud of a rawhide-booted hoof striking stone sounded from somewhere beyond the frail perimeter of the firelight.

The appaloosa tossed its head and the campfire was reflected in the moist jewels of its eyes as the animal stared off in the direction of that faint intrusion of sound. The blanket-shrouded figures did not stir. The big horse stamped nervously. Then there was nothing to be heard but the faint swishing of the water and the whirring beat of wings as an owl sped overhead, hunting.

A brief silence followed before that vagrant wind lifted once more, and as though boosted forward from behind by some invisible force, three grey-garbed figures ghosted out of the shadows into the dim fire glow.

The Mexicans wore no spurs and raised no sound at all as they cat-footed into the camp. For they were veterans of the wilder places of the South-West where they customarily plied their murderous trade.

Firelight glinted on naked gun barrels and sorrel features alike with a soft yellow sheen. The fire popped and the intruders halted sharply, eyes locking upon the sleeping figures. The blankets remained still and the night comers padded forward again until they could feel the warmth of the feeble flames upon their faces.

Salazar Hernandez halted them with a silent gesture and studied the faint outlines of the two tethered horses. His eyes glittered with greed. Quality horseflesh, the very best. Saddles and harness were also excellent, he could see, certainly far above the standards common to this benighted region.

Licking his lips the tall bandido returned his attention to the sleeping figures. He hunkered down by the nearer shape with his cocked six-gun almost touching the Stetson concealing the tall sleeper's head. He grinned like a dog wolf and and murmured softly:

'Señor gringo.'

No response.

Hernandez spoke louder. 'Awaken gringo scum, you have company!'

Still neither blanket stirred.

A momentary uncertainty flicked across the outlaw's features. He uncoiled sharply to his feet and poked a blanket with his toe. There was a faint sound like rattling sticks. Darting a puzzled glare look at his henchmen, Hernandez bent and ripped the blanket away.

At one end of the carefully arranged pile of brush and twigs that was arranged to approximate the size and shape of a human body, was placed a rock the size of a sleeper's head, covered by a Stetson.

The killer's eyes rolled bright and sick in their sockets. What the hell was this? He wanted to leap back, suddenly needed to run, yet his cowardly legs appeared to have locked up treacherously on him. Frozen and uncomprehending in back, his henchmen stared bug-eyed at him as though waiting for him to explain what in hell was going on.

They could see now by the very motionlessness of the second shrouded shape that it was also nothing but a lifeless dummy.

'You scum looking for us?'

The voice carried hard and cartridge-clear from the clump of pale rocks crowding the southern perimeter of the campsite. As one, the Mexicans whirled, juggling their revolvers as they stared wildly for a target.

'Drop those guns!'

Clay Rogan barely raised his voice, yet it carried. The three guntippers whirled as one to see nothing at all in the surrounding gloom but a deadfall log with one end propped up against the boulders. 'Do as I say or you're dead – make the choice!'

The disembodied voice carried steely authority. Shaking like an aspen in a high wind, Morelli dropped his .44 instantly, while the deadly Hernandez's gaunt face knotted with terrible indecision. But the reaction from runty Miguel Carrizo was to see him immediately explode into one of his famous rages.

'No – don't!' shouted Pinky Gist from the darkness when he saw what the loco hardcase meant to do.

Too late.

There was no halting Carrizo the slaughterman. Slipping into a low crouch the lightning shootist instantly cut loose with two fast shots that fanned lethally close to Gist's flat brim. In response, scarlet gun blasts streaked from Rogan's position and the outlaw reeled backwards jerkily for two slow steps. He clawed feebly at his chest where bright blood bubbled through his fingers. Somehow he squeezed off another shot. Hernandez's six-gun chimed in to support him and Morelli went diving wildly for his discarded Colt. Lethal gunfire poured out of the darkness and with his skull bursting open Carrizo went down, his going merely a soft rustle against the earth.

Hernandez did not see his henchman fall as he plunged wildly for the darkness, shooting back over one shoulder as he ran.

A fusillade of bullets smashed him off his flying feet. and Pablo Morelli shrieked like a woman in pure terror. He made as if to hurl his weapon aside, changed his mind, squeezed of one wild shot and died in a thunderclap of Colts.

Somehow a bloodied Hernandez rolled himself over and rose to hands and knees with his smoking cutter still in his shaking hand. The man could see nothing, heard nothing, just knew he was dying. But such was his ferocious nature he had to get off just one last shot. His gun roared and the bullet furrowed earth mere inches before him. A fusillade of gun thunder erupted from the darkness and he fell face down upon the earth, one foot stuttering to sudden stillness.

Two ghostly figures rose from the gloom, Pinky Gist short and stocky, Clay Rogan tall and broad.

Gist grinned as he came to stand above the remains of Morelli.

'Just had to buck the odds, didn't you, small-time. And it wasn't like you wasn't warned, now was it? You knew us Fort boys was coming to get you, yet you still had to buck the odds. I can tell you that—'

'Why don't you bottle it, mister?'

Gist swung sharply in surprise. Moving into the faint fire glow, Rogan looked as grim as any hangman.

'Hell, Roge, just letting off a little steam. I mean, they could have cut us down—'

'But they didn't. C'mon, let's go.'

'Go? But, man, we've got to get their documents and suchlike to prove we really bagged these bounty boys before the marshals will pay out on our claim.'

'We're getting the hell out of here, mister. No documents, no stinking claims – I'm gone!'

The runty bounty-hunter's jaws dropped. Let 'em lie? Big Rogan had been acting kind of strange this manhunt, he thought. But tossing away the best part of a thousand bucks? That was plain loco.

He said as much but his words were swallowed by the smoke-shrouded darkness.

It was a testing moment for Pinky Gist from Fort Such. The dead strewn about him in the dim firelight at this nameless bend in Salt River, were worth hard cash bounties and he was already envisioning himself living it up and playing the part of the big hero-winner to the hilt in front of his envious brother guns when they got back.

Yet after cussing like a mule skinner and kicking viciously at a rock, he found himself tramping off in Rogan's wake, leaving the peaceful dead behind.

Trouble was, a man got so used to doing whatever a top gun like Rogan or Silver said, you just naturally buckled under whether it made sense or not.

He caught up with Rogan as he was adjusting the cinch strap on his appaloosa stallion.

'Don't start!'

Any warning from Rogan packed weight and this was no different. But flashy Pinky's reaction was. This time. For failure to take back proof of their triple kill, in order to be able to claim their reward, would really hurt. He was flat busted and owed just about every-body back at the Fort – yet the solution to that was so simple it really hurt.

'Look, Clay, the least you can do is explain to a man what—'

'I didn't say you can't claim,' Rogan chopped him off. 'Just that I'm not. And I'm getting the hell and gone away from here just as soon as I swing one leg across this saddle.'

'But – but can't you just tell a man why you're so all-fired eager to turn your back on six hundred dollars' bounty? Is that asking too much?'

Rogan was about to lift boot to stirrup. He paused, then dropped his foot. He and Pinky Gist went back a ways. He figured the man at least rated an explanation. And who could tell? Maybe it would make his strange decision a little clearer even to himself while he was about it.

'All right,' he growled. He extended his hand. 'Give me one of those lousy stogies first. I need steadying down some.'

Gist's eyes bugged. Clay Rogan needed 'steadying down?' Was this some kind of joke?

It was no joke. Rogan took his time lighting up. He took several deep draws and stared back in the direction of the showdown scene before he spoke again. His voice was quiet, strange-sounding.

'Did you see their faces?'

Gist blinked. 'You mean them greasers? Hell, man they were just dead and—'

'I've had enough of this trade, Pinky,' the big man cut in. 'I've felt it coming on for quite a time, but reckoned I'd outride it. I meant to take those back-shooting sons of bitches alive if I could, claim on them and then sit down and do some serious think-

11

ing about the future. But when they doubled back on us that way they gave us no choice. But watching them go down I finally knew I'd killed once too often just for the dollar.' He snapped his fingers. 'So, I'm quitting.'

'Great Judas Iscariot, I don't believe what I'm hearing! What the hell will you do? You can't go straight – the John Laws would bag you and string you up in a minute. And it's no good of you moving on to another territory on account you and every one of us from the Fort has got wanted paper out on us all over every place—'

'You're not telling me anything I don't know, mister,' he cut in. He paused, then added thoughtfully, staring off: 'But there is a way. . . .'

'Sure!' Gist's tone was sarcastic. 'Jump a ship to Rio and lie around in the sun talking jig language and getting fat—'

'Amnesty!'

Pinky Gist's jaw dropped. 'Amnesty? You mean that latest piece of double-talking buffalo dust coming out of Capital City what promises that geezers like us can just mosey on up there, put in a claim to have our slate wiped clean by that double-dealing governor, take a soft job with the law, then just settle back nice and peaceful to grow old and fat like regular folks? *That* amnesty?'

Clay Rogan's face resembled something carved from stone as he swung up and settled into his saddle.

'That's the one I'll be looking for, pilgrim. Coming or staying?'

Pinky Gist cussed a blue streak as he stood indecisively staring back at the campsite. When he turned back it was to see Rogan swing up and head off into the gloom. For maybe a full twenty seconds the gunman stood motionless, locked in the worst indecision of his life. Yet eventually, seemingly helplessly, he then found himself jumping astride and kicking off in the other's dust.

Loyalty dominated him in that bitter moment, yet he had rarely been more angered either by a situation or his own weak-kneed response to it.

The veteran had reckoned he knew all the gross and ugly words a man might hear, yet the one that sounded worst of all had only gained currency over recent months in troubled Southwest County.

He simply couldn't believe gunman Clay Rogan could bring himself to utter that word much, less threaten actually to go seeking for something called . . . *amnesty*!

Lazy days in old Fort Such. . . .

The Fort had been something once back in the early days when the first post-war westbounders came flooding down into the beckoning South-West and everything that met the eye was new and exotic and garnished brilliantly by the light of their own high expectations, and something that was almost but not quite innocence.

Gone were the days.

By the time the Indians and Mexicans realized the main objective of every single brave and venturesome former citizen of New York, Charleston, South

Carolina or old Kentucky was to claim every acre, plain, mountain, river and sweeping panorama stretching to the horizon between Kansas and California as their very own – it was too bad for the original owners.

That had been the dream. Yet by now there were already too many dead, maimed and embittered down here for the vaunted 'New South-West' to be seen as anything other than which it had now largely become.

A war zone.

Few actually referred to it as that. Yet every 'visionary' explorer, empire-builder, official and peace-keeper – along with every embittered native of the regions – knew that was what it really was, and reacted accordingly.

Forts and outposts sprang up all over, while cattlemen and businessmen hired droves of gunmen to protect their 'acquisitions' from Apaches and people who spoke Spanish.

The gains here were huge, the risks frightening, the death count a matter of public shame. But there were always more than enough who believed it all worth it. And while some strongholds of the newcomers survived and grew more powerful and secure with time, just as many settlements were wiped off the face of the earth, or wound up like Fort Such.

Fort Such had served a ten-year term as a genuine army outpost bathed in blood in the early pioneering days, yet had lost its capability, integrity and general usefulness a full decade ago now.

No troopers trod the Fort's deadly streets any

longer, and yet the Fort and its littered surrounds were anything but deserted in these post-bellum days.

Although slowly but surely fading into decay and eventual oblivion and with its lethal population less than half it had been in its prime years, the Fort still attracted a certain breed of deadly citizen. And why not? Without one uniform, a five-pointed star or even an alcoholic preacher to be sighted within fifty miles of this sun-blasted spot standing roughly at the heart of Chisum Desert, it still provided a haven for every loser, killer, wife-beater, failed empire-builder, badman, drunk or fallen woman from a region one-third the size of Kentucky.

Any man or woman could act just as wild, independent, rebellious or downright criminal as they might want to down here. At times it had seemed impregnable yet not any more. It was only in recent months that lawless Fort Such, Chisum Desert, was uncharacteristically shaken to its collective boot-straps. Not by threats from the law, the Army, even the US Government itself – just something as seemingly harmless as a single word.

'Amnesty . . . anyone?'

Kip Silver liked to shock. It was a habit he'd picked up over time to fill in those silences that often greeted his return from one of those far-flung places where he plied his gun trade, all the way back to here, the place, the tiny lost outpost that the lethal, the lonesome and the truly lost still called home.

Fort Such.

Scarred gunfighters and a scatter of dangerous women drinkers forced grins to convince the new arrival now standing at Charron's Bar that they detected both the humour and irony in his mocking greeting, even if they didn't. Others just stared stony-faced, not game to rile the new arrival openly yet at the same time unwilling to pander to him on such a sensitive topic as this, either.

Genuine humour and irony were rarely encountered here at Charron's Bar, Fort Such. Owner Charron, whose real name was unknown and who'd selected his alias from a passage of the Bible, considered himself something of a wit and rangeland philosopher yet would never be mistaken for either. But clients down on their uppers often laughed immoderately at his efforts in the faint hope of alcoholic reward.

Silver looked disgusted as he rested an elbow on the bartop. Nobody knew where he'd come from tonight, only that he'd been away several days. The killer was neatly dressed and clean shaven, just like always. He was rarely ever sighted any other way down here in the desert lands of Southwest County.

'You know, Char, old crow bait, it beats me how tolerably tough geezers like some of your flock here can get to act so jittery just on account some dude up at the capital comes up with one itty-bitty dumb word backed up by some snake-oil scheme to put us down once and for all – damned if it don't. Why? Well, on account we all know it adds up to a dumb trick to sucker us in and then close your place down and land as many of us on the gallows or in county jail as they can muster. I mean, after all, you've seen it all before. Right? Old gunslinger like you?'

That was sarcasm and everybody in the place recognized it as such. For while Charron could boast all night long of his deeds with six-gun, knife and garrotte, it was widely known that the closest he'd ever come to a life of crime had been a five-year stint as a doorman at the biggest bordello in Capital City. That ignoble position had come to a messy end when he was caught stealing from a wealthy client, and barely escaped to his present life as bartender, philosopher and resident liar in the most dangerous drinking hole in Southwest Territory.

Charron just grinned at the remark. That could be wise whenever Kip Silver was involved. Silver had no friends here but there was rarely a man without good reason to fear him.

The saloon door opened suddenly to admit a harsh gust of sandy wind and a tall man with a bandanna drawn up over his nose against the Fort Such weather was boosted inside.

'OK, so I'm back!' the newcomer yelled, tugging down the bandanna to reveal the cocky, confident face of a young man with silver-blond thatch and laughing eyes. He struck a gunslinger's pose and slapped his Colt handles. 'And before anybody asks – he's dead and I ain't. Any questions?'

Someone laughed, another clapped spontaneously. For, dangerous though he was – as all were here – Danny Flynn was unusual insofar as he was naturally likeable. In a place like Charron's which catered to the killers, the lost, the wanted and those slowly drinking themselves to death before the law or their enemies beat them to it, this was an uncommon characteristic.

Flynn had the knack of making a six-gun massacre sound almost comical. He could even turn a typically dull and brooding night such as this in Fort Such into something almost enjoyable for those not too far gone to be able to enjoy anything any more.

'Howdy there, Kip old son,' the newcomer smiled, crossing the gritty floor and banging his high heels down hard to ensure everyone knew he was back. 'What you looking so cheerful about, anyway?'

Silver stood alone with his back against the bar, leaning on one elbow. Unlike most here, the man who shared the deadliest reputation of all looked more like an actor or an athlete than a man of the gun. Slimly built and fastidious about his appearance, he had a look almost of innocence about him which sometimes caused enemies to make the fatal mistake of underestimating him.

What Kip Silver lacked was charm, while the young man strolling across to the bar seemed loaded with it. This in itself was enough to rile Silver whilst puzzling most everyone else. Indeed, a gunslinger no longer living had once made the thoughtful comment, 'Everybody takes to Danny Flynn but Kip Silver.'

To be overtly disliked by Silver here or any place could be highly risky. But this danger was lessened where Flynn was concerned, the reason for this being about as simple as it could be. For there were just two gunmen who patronized this benighted place whom Silver was uncertain he could out draw. Danny Flynn was one, the other being absent at the moment.

The Kid sneered as he often did whenever he thought of Clay Rogan. He blanked his mind and offered a grudging nod. 'Always cheers me to see your smiling face, Danny boy. Hey, ain't that the name of a song?'

A sudden silence fell. All knew Flynn loathed being called 'Danny Boy'. Nobody here ever did so, with the exception of Kip Silver.

Safe behind his scarred bar Charron rubbed his nose and twitched visibly. For he was a coward who lived in constant fear of gunplay someday erupting here, where men wore guns as naturally as those in other places might wear hats against the sun.

He heaved a sigh of relief when Flynn just nodded with a 'one I owe you' glitter in his eye and drifted off to find romance or trouble, whichever might come easier on this windy night on the yellow dust plains.

Eventually weariness caught up with the saloon-keeper who settled into his favourite deep chair at the gloomy opposite end of the long bar with a flask of aged-overnight rum. He was soon beginning to doze and dream.

He didn't know how much later it was when he was jolted awake by sounds of violence. Blinking and cussing, he struggled to his feet to see two men whaling into one another in the centre of the saloon with fists, boots, knees and flying elbows.

He first cursed then sighed with relief when he realized it was just a couple of tenth-raters letting off steam. His first real fear was that it might be top-notchers such as Silver and Flynn, which might lead to anything.

He took down his shotgun from the rack above the bar and blasted a charge at the rear wall which was liberally scarred and pock-marked from similar incidents over time.

'That was one barrel!' he shouted as the brawlers sprang apart in alarm. He cocked the piece again, levelled it at them. 'You'll see the second in action if you don't simmer down and set – like right now!'

The two were newcomers to this grim dive in lonesome Fort Such. They didn't realize Charron lacked the grit to shoot a packrat. So they buckled under, sleeved the blood off their faces, grinned sheepishly and even managed to shake hands before retiring.

'So . . . what the tarnation was all that about?' demanded Charron, standing proudly tall in the wake of such a positive outcome. 'Or can I guess? Women?'

'Nah,' growled barfly Sundown Joe. 'Them boys are too smart to fall for that one. This was serious. Them boys got to discussing amnesty!'

'Shhh!' Charron warned, forefinger to lips. 'That is the one dirty word I never want to hear in my place. Ain't that so, Kip?'

'You're dead right there, old man!' Silver called from across the room. He rose from his table and stared challengingly around, his gaze cutting into every corner of the room. 'We don't hear that word and we don't speak it on account amnesty is just a name for Capital City's latest crummy scheme to turn us one against the other and then have us swallow the governor's sucker bait before winding up dead or on the gallows. Am I right, or am I right?'

The question was delivered at a shout which drew answering cheers which caused a thin film of dust to drift down from ancient rafters.

It was a fact of Southwest County life that the loners, fast guns and back-shooting killers who called this saloon home rarely felt threatened. Yet that single word, first sounded abroad just a matter of weeks earlier, had managed it.

For dangerous men it conjured up images of gunslingers turning traitor against their own kind. Of treachery, deception and even the eventual destruction of their bloody way of life.

Mutual agreement was always rare plains. But for once there appeared to be total unity concerning Governor Abel Fitzhenry and his latest attempt to clear up the 'blot' on his administration, which was the saloon at Fort Such.

After that tense moment, it developed into one of Charron's Bar's biggest nights where the drink flowed like spring water, dancing went on until the small hours and from time to time some two-gun-hellion or another was moved to jump upon a rickety table and deliver his personal denunciation of amnesty for gunslingers, its initiator up at Capital City, and any 'dirty sell-outs' who might be tempted to swallow Governor Fitzhenry's cunningly disguised bait.

There were just a few sore heads still abroad at false dawn when the most widely known fast gun of them all rode in to reveal he planned to travel north to Capital City and apply for amnesty.

Charron thought Clay Rogan was joking at first. When he realized the big man was dead serious his first fearful thought was that this could prove to be the first hole in the dam wall that might in time drown them all.

CHAPTER 2

LONE GUN RIDING

Rogan reined in and stared back.

Nothing.

No sign of a slowly rising dust cloud that could indicate somebody on his trail. Just mile upon mile of sun-stricken desert dotted here or there by a skinny red butte or hill of sand. And finally, no sign of the ugly blot on the landscape that was the town of Fort Such, now far behind. Nor yet a first glimpse of the mountains which he must cross to gain the high plateau which then stretched all the way to Capital City.

He massaged his clean-shaven jaw then used up a further minute rolling and lighting a smoke. No big hurry, he told himself. Speed was not an essential factor when travelling Chisum Desert, Southwest County. Stamina was all that counted here. At times he'd heard himself being compared to this country – hard and demanding.

And the back of his mind seemed to whisper, 'And maybe a tad crazy?'

He grimaced and drew deep. Maybe so. Some back at Fort Such seemed convinced he'd lost his head if he genuinely expected Governor Fitzhenry would wave the wand of forgiveness and renewal over his bowed head, should he turn himself in. Danny Flynn had even drunkenly insisted he and Rogan make their final goodbyes, convinced that the moment he showed his face on the streets of the capital the governor would first throw the net over him then holler for his hangman.

Fitzhenry well might do just that. Yet Rogan doubted it. He'd investigated the amnesty proposal as far as he was able. There were publicized instances of gunmen and outlaws applying for and being granted official forgiveness for their sins. He'd seen the records. So why not him? He should not be discriminated against simply because he was renowned as being some kind of figurehead at Fort Such. Should he?

He banged heels against horsehide and rode on. He knew he would feel more relaxed now had he been able to thrash things out with Kip Silver before leaving. But the gunslinger was off shacked up some-place with one of Charron's girls and nobody had been able to find him before he quit town.

Silver wasn't going to like it when he heard. There was little that Kip did like, while boasting a long list of dislikes such as authority, fast gun-rivals, the law, government, the emancipation of women – the list was endless. At the present his pet hate was amnesty.

'Too bad,' Rogan muttered, causing his mount to prick its ears. 'Maybe I'll find it's not for me either – but I'm still at least going to find out. . . .'

He didn't dwell on his future should he fail to secure amnesty. He would never be trusted by the Fort Such brotherhood again; Silver and others like him would see to that. Maybe he would just keep pushing west until he reached someplace where nobody had ever heard of him, then take up chicken ranching?

He smiled, something he rarely did. That was a real stretch for his imagination. Clay Rogan – rancher? He could not see it. Seriously, he figured something maybe connected to the law or security might work out best.

The miles flowed behind, the silence almost dreamlike. There were few landmarks here. He didn't need them. His innate sense of direction kept him on a north-by-north-west course as surely as if he had a compass set in the swell fork pommel of his saddle.

The terrain slowly changed again, growing rougher and uglier before the higher country ahead. It was as he approached the first of the rugged rock-bench slopes which led on to the brushy hog-back ridges and deep-cut canyons, that he glimpsed a faint spiral of dust rising above his back trail.

A short time later he located a patch of shade, swung down, watered the horse from his canteen, and settled down to wait.

He knew who it was; who it had to be.

The first time he'd camped here he had clambered up that towering rock slab yonder and spent two hours of moonlight atop it just drinking in the nocturnal landscape. He recalled that night as one that marked a great change in his life. Up until then he had been more like some kind of idealist, even if a dangerous one in many ways. But a short time prior, he'd lost a close pard in a gun battle with the Osages up in Kansas, and it seemed that incident had caused the iron to enter his soul.

That, and Kathy.

She was his first love, likely the last. She said she loved him then ran off to the East Coast with a traveller in household fittings.

He could smile at that recollection now. Up until that incident he'd had any number of romances and a few important-seeming love affairs. But the one time he had allowed himself to trust completely and be true, as men of his profession rarely were, he had been rejected in favour of a gentleman who sold taps, washers, dumb waiters and window screens.

At that time of his life the incident had hit hard. He always believed it was the reason he'd been able to be persuaded into going down to Mexico in pursuit of an escaper from Yuma pen.

His quarry almost escaped by seeking cover in a Sonoran revolution. By the time he'd survived that war, and spent three months in a one-room hospital recovering from an undiagnosed fever before tracking down his man, Rogan had matured into a hard man with a quick gun and a restlessness that continued to make itself felt today.

He returned to Arizona as a dedicated manhunter

and gunfighter and had seen no good reason to change – until four days ago. That brutal shootout at Riata Creek was the incident which starkly drove home the full understanding of what he had allowed himself to become. He'd been lucky to survive that set-to, was now totally resolved to seek some way to shed his gunslinger rep and hopefully find a new way to travel on without dead men dotting his wake.

But first he must deal with that rider kicking up dust behind. If it was who he figured, then he was as dangerous as anybody he'd ever known. He saw the pursuer was drawing closer by the minute now.

Yet he still found himself able to relax in the peace and pleasure of the moment as he gazed out over the shadow-rumpled desert, studded in the far distance of the green south with grazing buffalo.

A stranger dumped here could believe himself to be a thousand miles from civilization, whereas in fact it was less than forty miles to the territorial capital and his appointment with the governor.

If he made it.

Common sense said that thought must enter a man's head at a time like this. Yet it irked him. He rose and went pacing restlessly about the gaunt landscape until dusk and Kip Silver arrived together.

By then he was back at his campsite fixing vittles over a low fire. Hunkered there he appeared a picture of outdoor ease and contentment, but inside was wound up tighter than an eight-day clock.

The gunman rode up and halted, waiting for him to speak first. Clay just glanced his way then returned his attention to his skillet. Silver liked to rattle people, felt it gave him an edge. The gunslinger appeared belligerent as he finally slid to ground and hitched up his shell belt. He was neat and tidy, just like always. Rogan was conscious of the power of the man's presence. A man might hate the Kipper but it could be suicidal to take him lightly.

After what seemed a long time, Kip Silver found himself forced to speak first.

'Is it true?'

'Sure. I'm applying for amnesty.'

'You Judas sonofa—' the other began. He bit off the words and sucked in a deep breath. 'You know, Lonely, a certain kind of man could read that as selling out to the common enemy. And that could make this here certain kind of man see red. You understand what I'm saying – big man?'

Rogan uncoiled to full height in one unhurried motion. He inhaled, relying upon superior height and size to intimidate. He was unsuccessful. Silver was a little over average height with a muscular slenderness of physique. He never attempted to make himself appear big. His superiority lay in a pair of .45s.

'I'll lay it on the line, Rogan. I see what you're planning on doing as betraying the Fort, the boys, everything we stand for. While deadwoods like Fitzhenry make speeches and rattle their sabres at the likes of us, we go on living just the way we want and don't run from nobody. That's how we are, and that's the reason I came after you. To tell you none of us boys believe in any stinking amnesty. That we're not going to get down on our knees and crawl to any stinking governor – and think mighty poorly of any man who might. You hear me good – Lonely?'

'You were always loud enough, Kid,' Rogan said quietly. He didn't care for the 'Lonely' tag any more than Silver liked being called 'Kid.'

They'd been natural enemies from day one but it was never this serious before. You could almost smell the gunsmoke.

'OK, you made your spiel and I heard you out. I'm still going to Capital City.' He paused for emphasis. 'To find out about amnesty and if it suits, apply for it. So, how's *your* hearing?'

A sly wind whispered in the thornbrush and somewhere far off a whippoorwill sounded.

They stood facing in fading light, two men so very much alike, yet vitally different. Both lived by the gun and lived well because of their talent. That was the similarity, the solitary one. In every other way that counted they were opposites.

Despite a daunting manner and borderline arrogance, big Rogan attracted people ranging from mining tycoons to fifth-rate guntippers living on the fringes in Fort Such.

By marked contrast, few people cared for Kip Silver, which was largely his fault. Even in Fort Such where gun skill was held in higher regard than money, women, fame or glory, this star shootist could claim but one genuine friend. But as Jorgan Kroll was so poisonous and treacherous by nature, he didn't really seem to count.

Another man might have found such isolation burdensome. Not Silver. His vaulted opinion of himself kept him warm nights. He valued neither associations, friendships or lovers. Colt supremacy and all that went with it comforted him and made him strong.

Silver was never lonely, never in need, had not once in his life fretted about what anyone might think of him. He rode this brutal land alone like some kind of knight errant of the six-guns, and lesser men could only look on with envy and bad mouth him only when drunk or simply when they did not care any longer.

Rogan knew all this and was therefore taken aback when the killer's manner underwent a dramatic change.

'Clay,' he said amiably, and the use of his given name was free of his usual mockery. 'Look at us. We are the same. We're kings of the freaking county and just about write our own tickets, if we want. This place is facing its biggest challenge over this lousy amnesty deal, there's going to be bloodshed and fortunes won and lost. And sooner or later, both of us are going to be sucked into the ruckus on account those tall poppies from the capital ain't going to be able to get by without us. Then we'll be able to name our own price – could wind up richer than even the freaking railroad or the Cattle Combine – or Fitzhenry, his stuffed-shirt self. You know what I'm saying?'

'Better spell it out for me.'

'We pard up, of course. Look at the headlines; Silver and Rogan team up! Lock up your daughters and run for cover, all you government stuffed shirts, you lousy colonels with your gold braid – and just stand back and watch the so-called 'gunfighters' suddenly disappear as the two men with the power end up deciding just which way this territory is heading!'

He paused to throw his hands wide, smiling as he so rarely did, eyes glitter-bright in the dusk.

'Well?'

Rogan was genuinely surprised. But not one whit touched or tempted, not even for the shaved tip of a moment.

'See you, Kid.'

Silver went white. 'What?'

'Sure I'm taking a chance, going to the capital looking for amnesty. I could get thrown into jail, maybe hanged. But I'm still going, still mean to put it to the test. What I'm saying is that I'd sooner wind up swinging off that gibbet in the yard behind the governor's palace than throw in with you, and that's just the simple truth.'

He anticipated outrage, maybe even a lightning two-handed grab for six-guns in those explosive seconds which followed.

But Kip Silver could always surprise, as Rogan realized when the gunslinger simply nodded slowly and touched fingertips to hatbrim. He turned his back and vaulted up over his horse's rump with the agility of an acrobat to land neatly in the saddle.

He was gone in a moment leaving behind a sluggish cloud of dust and the memory of one backward stare which seemed almost to sear the skin.

Rogan attempted to grin to prove he was

unmoved. He failed. The reality was, that final rift with Silver, always on the cards, had plainly finally come.

He took out his cigars and made a slow deliberate business of peeling off the wrapper, piercing the end with a matchstick, lighting up, more aware than ever of his status.

Until that moment he'd been totally preoccupied with amnesty and what he might have to do to achieve it. Had considered the changes he must make to succeed and the inherent danger for a man committed to changing his horses in the mid-stream of his life.

Now suddenly his mind was calm and blank.

He'd intended resting up here at the spring. He was weary, the horse was footsore and the desert cold was already creeping in. Yet within minutes he was saddled up and pushing into the north-west beneath a sea of stars. It was a long time before he could overcome that instinct to hip around suddenly in his saddle to see if somebody might be stealing up from behind.

Nervousness was something totally new for him. Like amnesty.

The final official document had been signed, the last whining applicant sent on his way – unhappy and disgruntled no doubt. And for a few rare and precious minutes the most powerful man in the territory found himself alone, at peace and relaxed.

He frowned, then shook his head. No. Not really relaxed. He had not been that way since making the official decision to bring forward and resolve at last the pressing application by the Great Southwest Railroad Company to string steel from Rebel River to Capital City.

The governor grimaced and pressed fingers to the corners of his eyes. Without thinking, he lifted his head and called; 'George, advise Mrs Fitzhenry I'm free at last, will you?'

He stopped and swore softly even before the door opened a crack and assistant Watson poked his head around the frame.

'Sorry, Governor, Mrs Fitz—'

'I know, I know . . . I just forgot for a moment.' Sarcasm gripped him. He made a grimace. 'At the gardens? Or is it the Women's Auxiliary tonight?' His tone was sarcastic. He made a sweeping gesture with his right hand. 'Never mind – never damn well mind. I suppose this means I shall be dining alone again tonight?'

'Er, well, if you would like my wife and me to join you, sir, we'd be only too—'

'Thank you, George, but I'm so played out I'd be poor company.' He made a dismissive gesture. 'Tell your good lady eggs will suffice. Eggs for one, that is.'

'For one? Yes, sir.'

The door closed and the governor rose and stretched, a tall lean-bodied man with the upright carriage of the cavalryman he'd once been. Still vigorous and impressive at fifty, Governor Abel Fitzhenry had only recently fallen into the habit of studying his reflection in mirrors as he passed, searching for physical signs of his weariness which

33

seemed to be growing greater with each day.

He knew he'd both feel and function far better were his wife less preoccupied with her many extracurricular affairs, and was more involved with life here at the governor's mansion atop the hill over-looking Capital City. Yet that situation certainly showed no sign of change nor promise of improvement.

He stepped out onto his balcony to see the lights of the sprawling plateau town laid out in a glittering carpet below.

His smile was cynical. The capital could appear almost attractive by night . . . but only then. Darkness concealed a multitude of imperfections. He knew only too well that down there was to be found sin, vice, violence and corruption seemingly without limit. Yet to be fair he'd also discovered much that was good and promising out here on the frontier – lying so far, so very far from the East where he'd been born and raised in those good years before the finest nation on earth got to tear itself apart.

He grimaced.

Bring in the army! That had been the cry back then, and some were now even advocating the same 'cure' here in the South-West for the troubles that beset them.

He'd been opposed to the War between the States but that certainly hadn't mattered a toss. Pretty soon he was drawn into it, and even now, standing here on his high balcony waiting for a manservant to bring him his evening gin and bitters, the memories could still reach out and grab him. Shiloh, Blake's Woods,

Tennessee Junction and the whole murderous madness of the Shenandoah campaign. Leading his troops cleverly and well even though they were finally destined to be rolled over by Stonewall Jackson's foot soldiers – who also believed in 'Bring in the army!'

Yet even after all that endless horror, men still believed war was the way to solve things. When he'd first proposed a blanket amnesty for rustlers, outlaws and all those other malcontent survivors from both sides of the great war out here, there were cries of outrage along with calls for his dismissal, and for his office here to be replaced by the army.

That would only ever happen over his dead body. He knew his methods might seem extreme and even reckless to many, but he would not change. With this rich rangeland plateau now almost a war zone of claim and counter-claim regarding ownership of contested or unbranded stock, and power-grabbing cattlemen hiring private armies of gunmen to protect themselves and their ambitions, it had only taken the final element of the railroad to tip the uncertain balance here towards disaster.

The governor would not countenance failure, however. He was on the verge of signing the authority to the Great Southwest Railroad to string its twin steel ribbons across the final twenty miles to the capital from Larribee, the main purpose of which, from the governor's point of view, would be to smash finally the iron grip the cattlemen had held for too long over the territory and its fledgling capital.

Here, the cattleman was still king. And while ever land title, stock ownership and relevant matters were in such confusion, authority could be exploited by the 'haves', or the cattlemen or virtually everybody else associated with mining, business, politics. And, of course, the poor. . . .

A man of vision if not subtlety, Fitzhenry foresaw the railroad opening up the entire country and hurrying the rationalization of land titles, thus hastening the final break-up of the ruthless and corrupt dynasty notoriously known as the Cattle Combine.

Naturally the Combine would resist and it was this factor more than any other which had first prompted the governor to begin implementing amnesty for outlaws, gunmen and illegals from south of the border. His theory: give such men the chance to break away from their dependence upon the warring ranchers and start out afresh, and surely the whole region could not help but improve, pacify and eventually get to shape a more stable and progressive future.

It was proving a huge gamble, and failure would spell his own end. But having begun he would forge ahead, hammer home his reforms, by force if necessary. And then take any extreme step he considered justified, such as the amnesty programme and the completion of the railroad, at last again under construction.

And to hell with his critics!

His drink arrived on time and he relaxed in his favourite chair reviewing in his mind yet again the overarching situation Washington expected him to rectify.

Cattle and cattle problems dominated the Capital City region and had done for far too long. In their earlier boom days the cattle kings had branded anything they could rope and to hell with legalities. While fighting savagely amongst themselves they had still managed to grow rich through wholesale rustling, brand-blotting and overriding any attempts to clarify what appeared to be an insoluble mess, from an administratior's point of view.

Fitzhenry had struggled for over a year to make sense of the situation, before finally hitting upon his ruthless if eminently straightforward solution.

Forget the power and brutality of the Cattle Combine – for resolution of the ownership and title of so many thousands of stock was plainly impossible. The Combine herded their assembled stock overland to the railroad up at Larribee, and had the strength and ruthlessness to prevent the dozens of small cow ranchers around the capital from accessing that market. Yet the railroad, insisting upon proof of title from day one, had been operating successfully for some time now, boasting they never shipped a beeve with suspect ownership!

The line was already building to the west before they grew fully aware of the brand-ownership crisis in Southwest County, and had shelved plans to complete a twenty-mile spur line to Capital City until the situation there was settled. But it had remained unresolved until the day a suddenly enlightened governor summoned his inner cabinet and outlined his inspired solution: 'Finish the damned line and from there on the railroad will bring in and ship out only legally branded stock, thereby building up the small ranchers and ultimately reducing the Combine to sell their suspect stock into Sonora for peanuts as long as they damn well like!'

It was *still* a great idea. The governor was working day and night ironing out the problems with its implementation. In so doing he'd alienated himself from his long-suffering wife and triggered off what felt like the onset of a stomach ulcer. Even so, he was more committed to his plan of resolution now than at its conception.

But storm clouds were gathering. The Combine was threatening action both legal and otherwise while the railroad was frantically resuming construction to complete what could prove to be the most profitable section of its north-west line. And the governor didn't sleep soundly any longer.

As if all that was not enough for one man at one time! Now he was expected to deal with the arrival of one of those gunmen from the desert applying for amnesty!

He was considering a second drink when a sharp rap sounded on the balcony door and his official aide strode in without waiting for permission to enter.

That was typical of Rade Tierney, Fitzhenry brooded. He was a man in a hurry and as such paid little attention to the amenities either here at the mansion or anyplace else. Some found his style forceful and stimulating, but many saw the fellow as rude and arrogant.

'Well, he's on his way,' was the deputy's greeting. 'Just got a wire from the south-east.'

'Oh yes?' the governor replied calmly, studying his glass. 'And who would that be?'

The younger official placed hands on hips and drilled a hard stare on his superior.

Rade Tierney was rangy, lean and hard. He looked more like a military man or outdoorsman than a young official on his way up the ladder. His wedge-shaped face was tanned and taut, there was a sense of swagger in every movement. A product of the war and a former political strategist in the East, he'd been promoted and assigned duty in the territory by a relative with political pull in Washington.

The governor did not think highly of his deputy, and vice versa. They were men of divergent views. Yet both were energetic and forward-looking and had made the best of their uneasy liaison. That was, until the Combine-railroad-amnesty problems had reared their heads, resulting in ever-deepening variances of opinions and objectives, and friction.

Tierney was opposed both to amnesty and the completion of the railroad spur line, both Fitzhenry initiatives. The deputy wished to assign the army the responsibility of cleaning out the outlaw haunts and ridding the fledgling territory of notorious gunfighters roosts such as Capital City and Fort Such, reforms which the governor had used his authority to oppose totally. Tierney was also fighting against the governor's concessions to the railroad with all he had, thus far to no noticeable advantage.

Small wonder their meetings were growing more rare and strained as the summer marched towards an early fall.

There were papers to be signed, which the governor attended to while the other paced to and fro. As Tierney was restless by nature, once the paperwork was completed Fitzhenry expected him to make his departure with the minimum of formalities.

When the fellow lingered, thoughtful-looking and tapping his sleeve with the envelope, the governor took another leisurely sip, then cocked an eyebrow.

'Something else?'

The man's gaunt face hardened. 'Matter of fact, there is.' He paused a moment, then added with a touch of spite. 'He's coming.'

'And who might that be? Johnny Appleseed, perhaps?' The spirits were getting to him. He was aggravated by his wife's absence as much as by his deputy's presence. Tonight, he would enjoy brooding alone, maybe even get a little drunk. After all, he was governor and could do whatever he damn well liked.

'Very amusing—' the other began, then bit off his words. The aide felt reasonably secure here, despite their differences. But it never paid to forget that the governor could cancel his well-paid contract at the drop of a hat, should he choose. He reached inside his jacket pocket and produced a newspaper clipping featuring a grainy photograph, passed it to his superior.

'Good likeness, Governor, wouldn't you say? He quit Fort Such day before yesterday, should be here any time now.'

Fitzhenry studied the clipping. It showed a man, impressively tall and broad, standing before a horse.

Both man and beast appeared aloof. The man wore two revolvers on his hips and his expression was a blend of arrogance and intelligence.

The governor realized Clay Rogan had changed some since they last met. The gunman did not necessarily appear older, but something had altered about him. Maybe he had tamed down some, he speculated, although he supposed that was hardly likely. He was forced to concede the Fort Such man did not appear noticeably any the less dangerous since they had met briefly and for the first time some six months earlier.

'No comment, Governor?'

'What would you like me to say, Deputy? The more the merrier? Or perhaps—'

'You can't seriously mean to grant amnesty to that one?' Tierney demanded. 'It would be like setting a rogue bull loose on a milk farm. You—'

'Good night, Mr Tierney.'

Tierney stared. He was being dismissed. Colour flushed flat cheeks. He made to retort but changed his mind. He took the clipping with him as he strode out, slamming the door behind him.

The governor's wry smile was short lived. He rang the bell and waited for his manservant to appear and pour him another, then dismissed him. He carried the glass to the balcony railing where he stood sipping at it, his gaze fixed thoughtfully upon the south-east.

He knew he was taking huge risks these days, opening the gates for the railroad antagonizing the ranchers, advocating amnesty as one possible if patently untried method of coping with the territory's lawlessness.

There had been a time when he would have been able to sit down with his wife and discuss such weighty matters, but she was hardly about any more, so it seemed.

He briefly considered visiting Lulu's on Peach Street, but it scarcely seemed worth the effort. Instead he settled into his deep chair, sipping from his glass and picturing the storm that would break over his grey head should his decision to offer amnesty to gunmen like Clay Rogan blow up in his face.

And finally slept, towards the end of summer.

CHAPTER 3

THE CRUEL LAND

He was a tired man at sundown as he reined in and sleeved the sweat off his face. He looked down at his water canteen, licking dry lips. But he didn't drink. He might well be heading for a new and softer way of life at the end of this journey, yet still old habits died hard. Early in life he'd learned that any gunfighter who planned to survive must of necessity make himself harder, stronger and more enduring than the next man if he planned to survive in the most dangerous trade of all.

So he would continue denying his simple body needs such as water or food, along with other life-time habits until certain this new life he was reaching for here reassured him he could afford to ease up some.

With the thought came another, unwelcome and yet undeniable. *That* easy day might never come. A tiger might change its stripes but some would argue it would remain a tiger until the day it died. That analogy transposed to himself suggested that, even should he seek the redemption of amnesty, he might always remain a gunman.

'Stop trying to cheer yourself up,' he grinned, causing the horse to toggle its ears. He patted the sweating neck, said, 'Water just up ahead,' and kneed the appaloosa forward.

And so crossed the breadth of the night to raise eventually the distant glow that were the lights of the city. He kept the glow between the horse's ears and the slow miles continued to fall behind.

It was force of long habit to keep glancing back over his shoulder. There was nothing out there and he didn't really expect there to be. But he'd known top guns who had been stalked and killed simply because they were arrogant and couldn't believe anyone would risk trying to steal up on them in the dark to give them six in the back.

Kip Silver did not enter his thinking. Sure, Silver was mad clear through and would be happy to dance on his grave following the 'act of treachery' Rogan was planning. The consoling factor was that should Silver ever come after him, Rogan knew death would not come with a bullet in the back from ambush. Not with Silver it would not. That shootist would have to face him and kill him fair, square and legal or else feel his pride and vanity forever traduced.

He brushed aside thoughts of Silver and Fort Such and speculated upon whatever might await him up ahead. He fashioned and smoked a cigarette and watched as the lights ahead began dying one by one.

He planned to reach his destination in the dead of night, which for wild Capital City never meant midnight but rather two or three a.m. For it was a roistering, racketing, trouble-plagued town where the law and the militiamen were kept busy day and night, yet never quite succeeded in keeping the violence or the death rate down to a halfway acceptable level.

Smiling cynically as the horse went grunting stiff-legged down a sandy draw, he remembered the newly installed governor's inaugural address. The gunner had happened to be present amongst the crowd that day, having just delivered a one-armed, one-legged stage bandit to the jailhouse for a two-hundred-dollar bounty.

'. . . A new day has dawned, my fellow citizens, and the old ugly days of this city's troubled hundred years are gone forever. Where fear once dominated, now you shall find peace and rule of law. No less a man than the governor of Arizona Territory selected me personally for this Homeric task and I swear to you I shall justify his confidence. I know I can rely upon each and every one of you to go forward with me on this great journey.'

Rogan shook his head.

So much for idealism and buffalo dust. Fitzhenry had fallen so far short of his objectives here that he was forced to have armed escorts accompany him whenever he left the compound. Now he was prepared to humble himself by offering amnesty to men like himself after realizing they could be neither killed nor controlled.

Yet, he supposed, he was lucky this was the situation. For if he hadn't had the prospect of amnesty and a paying job with the government here, what would his future be now? For a gunfighter, the enforcement of power and living cheek by jowl with danger was all he knew. He would be searching for work here should he secure amnesty, and doubtless it would have something to do with guns. Yet he hoped to alter his status here dramatically. Become something other than just another gunslinger sporting a badge. He wanted to ease out of the gun life, not prolong it.

It was a gamble, sure. But a gunslinger gambled with his life every day.

He could smell the city as he crossed the final flat stretch from the river to raise the first scatter of lean-tos on the southern fringes.

He straightened his back and willed away the weariness, every sense fully alert. Capital City knew he was coming; he'd made sure of that. He was taking the precaution of showing up at twenty-to-three in the dark of the night in the hope of avoiding trouble, yet he'd be six kinds of a fool to be anything but cautious in this place. There were men living here whom he'd shot, turned over to the authorities, hunted halfway across the county or simply beat up in saloon brawls. Any number of losers who might grab at a chance to get square. It would take time for that hellion breed to grow accustomed to the notion of sharing their hometown with Clay Rogan, and until that day came he would take no chances.

The appaloosa's hoofs rang hollowly as he crossed the little bridge on the capital's west side, but tossed its head with relief as they followed the first rutted street which led through the westside slums, lifting its gait just a little in anticipation of rest, water and grain.

With a crimson cigarette tip glowing dimly in the shadow of his sombrero, the rider sat easy in his saddle but his gaze missed nothing. He saw where someone had ditched a handcart in a gutter, noted the night wind flapping washing on a string line over by that barn with the busted roof.

The city slept, or so it would seem.

The closer he worked his way towards the plaza square the more starlight was blotted out by high-rising warehouses, tenements of pinewood and mud and the occasional storeroom with massive padlocks securing the scarred doors.

All was silent. He began to relax some before he rounded a gloomy corner where he instantly drew the horse to a sharp halt.

Standing hipshot in an alley mouth some distance to his right were the dark outlines of a pair of saddle ponies, long-maned and head-hanging in the silence.

In a moment, his right hand filled with gun. In the next, he swung down, looped the reins over a fence post and went stalking forward, making not a breath of sound.

A pair of tethered ponies was nothing to get excited about. Unless of course a man happened to encounter them in the dark of the night in a commercial back alleyway where there seemed no legitimate reason for their presence – other than the one that had struck him the moment he first saw them.

Trouble? He could smell it.

He gained the nearest corner. He flattened his back against a wall and eased one eye around to stare down a littered alleyway piled high with packing crates and junk, beyond which could be seen the dim night lights of the square.

And much closer, crouched low enough to be almost invisible, two dim figures clutching six-guns and facing the alley he'd been traversing before stumbling upon their horses.

He proceeded to divest himself silently of hat, boots and gunbelt – anything that might make a sound. He dropped into a low crouch and snaked around his corner, leaning even lower as he closed in. They had their backs to him. He heard a muttered word in Mexican dialect, caught the whiff of unwashed bodies, stepped lightly over a sack of junk, then halted and straightened.

'Reach, scum!'

They jumped like startled deer, eyes rolling whitely in their sockets as they whirled to face a figure which appeared seven feet tall in their fear and surprise. The hawk-faced man dropped his gun but his companion was jerking his piece upwards when Rogan lunged swiftly forward and brought his right-hand gun over in a savage arc to smash the barrel across his face and send him spinning senseless to ground.

'*Por . . . por favor, señor. . . .*' the first man sputtered, but choked silent when the big gun rammed into his face. 'Pick him up and tote him to the square, wetback. Blink just once and I'll kill you both!'

That was how Clay Rogan arrived in Capital City, Southwest County. Not as he would have wished, maybe. But to those who knew him and of him, more or less what might have been expected.

The driver swung the surrey round the Peach Street corner with a flourish, drawing a sharp reproof from within the vehicle behind.

'We're taking a tour of inspection, Wilson, not competing in the National Derby!'

'Er, sorry, sir,' the man called back over his shoulder. 'Past the courthouse next?'

'If you must.'

'You don't want to stop by, Governor?'

'I most certainly do not.'

There was a small crowd assembled before the city courthouse as the stylish rig wheeled by at the trot. Someone cheered, another jeered. The governor acknowledged both formally then leaned far back against the soft leather cushions where he was invisible to the great unwashed as the equipage continued on its down the main street.

A preliminary hearing was taking place back at the courthouse today, Judge Michael Moran presiding. Fitzhenry knew he could rely on the judge to handle the case adroitly, which in his terminology meant Moran would find some reason to have the case of Lopez and Mondrega slotted in for hearing someplace else other than here – anyplace else.

There was good reason for that. Clay Rogan had not even checked in last night before clashing with a pair of abbattoir labourers who had drunk themselves into believing the Fort Such gunfighter had been brought in to ride roughshod over the Mexicans and Indians of the city, and so unwisely hatched up the idea for their own inept ambush.

As the governor viewed the incident, the pair might have been shot to doll rags without anybody being too concerned. In a way he wished they had been – but not by this man.

His man.

He turned the phrase on his tongue and scowled. There had been violent protests from a number of quarters when word was first released that Rogan would be considered as a candidate for amnesty. The most vociferous of these had come from the cattlemen and the poor, both elements being violently opposed to the many changes Fitzhenry had been introducing, rightly fearful of how they might impact on them.

As far as the governor was concerned both factions could go straight to hell. Unfortunately he would not dare admit to such sentiments for obvious political reasons.

He was touted as everybody's champion here, and that included lowlifes whom he privately considered should have been strangled at birth.

Even so, Abel Fitzhenry knew he would have felt far more relaxed today had the notorious Fort Such *pistolero* arrived quietly and without controversy. Had Rogan got to present his credentials formally at the mansion some time today without first having been involved in a ruckus that could well have ended in gunplay and death, might well have been desirable.

And Fitzhenry thought, not for the first time: 'Is attempting to draw their teeth and civilize them *really* a better policy than mustering all forces and trying to wipe all those Fort Such scum off the map as I've been advised by some. . . ?'

The surrey struck a pothole. The governor cursed irritably then reached forward with his cane to tap the driver on the shoulder.

'Take me to Poortown,' he shouted. 'And do try to miss one in ten chock holes, will you?'

'Got you, Governor! Er . . . the usual place, sir?'

'The usual place,' he growled. And tried to convince himself he was merely using up time to delay his eventual face-to-face with Rogan, while knowing deep down his real intention was to catch a glimpse of his estranged wife, surely the most difficult of all women in an increasingly difficult and complex world.

The governor was not always this negative. Yet if a man wanted to let himself feel that way, he brooded, Capital City, Southwest Territory was just the place for it.

He stared unseeingly from the windows watching the better houses quickly give way to the sprawling maze of shacks and hovels of Poortown. He wondered yet again just how long his period of political penance here would have to extend before he was promoted to a real town occupied by real people.

He brushed the thought aside. One thing was for

sure. He must succeed here before he could be certain of promotion and that long-anticipated boost upwards in administration rankings he so ardently craved.

Territorial headquarters had made no bones about the fact that his promotion to this office was based on a belief in his ability to achieve this feat of reconstruction.

That meant in particular succeeding in the rail-road-versus-cattlemen conflict while improving the level of law and order in the city. He conceded this might now largely depend upon his success or failure with his most high profile claimant yet for amnesty.

Someone hurled a can at the carriage and the governor cursed bitterly. It looked like being a long day.

The breakfast was fine but Rogan wasn't really hungry. Finally he shoved his plate away, signalled for a second mug of joe and lighted a cheroot.

Midge Riddle's place on Frontier Street was nothing special from outside but within proved to be surprisingly roomy and comfortable.

Midge, a tough mite of a woman who smoked a curved pipe, had greeted him, a total stranger, with the salutation, 'What'll it be, shooter?'

He'd had to grin. For some dumb reason he'd actually hoped he might get to drift into the capital more or less anonymously, set himself up, go to the mansion and investigate this amnesty business while playing down who he was and why he'd come.

What a joke!

He'd since learned that the dogs had been barking about his pending arrival long before he had shown up at the jailhouse just before dawn with two men held at gunpoint and demanding – not suggesting – both face trial for attempted murder.

In any event, it was not the end of the world. With his smoke going nicely he fished money from the slash pocket of his leather riding jacket and crossed to the counter.

'Somethin' wrong with my vittles, Sunny Jim?' he was challenged.

'Fit for a king, Midge. Guess I'm just off my chaff is all. How much?'

She leaned forward on bony elbows to study him at close range. 'That depends.'

'On what?'

'On the answer to the question everyone's askin' hereabouts. Which is – is the likes of you showin' up through the buffalo dust lookin' for this newfangled am-ness-tee goin' to make things better or worse hereabouts. That's what.'

'Why, worse, of course.'

She burst out laughing. 'Right answer. Go on, off you go. I got a hunch you might be able to pull something off here now I've had a chance to size you up. I got a free-meal hour Saturday night twixt seven and eight, and you're welcome. That's if you're still breathing, of course.'

Back on the street, Rogan took his thoughts for a walk.

It was no surprise to find the capital appeared far better at 10 a.m. than it had at four-in-the-morning.

There were still some fine old Spanish-style buildings standing, stately and proud, dating back to the Mexican days, before the huge western expansion post Civil War.

He encountered a city-like hustle and bustle along Main Street, and over on the plaza square, buggies, wagons and all manner of one- and two-horse rigs were noisily vying for right-of-way against huge-wheeled wagons, while flashy young bucks on their drafting ponies cut in and out of traffic.

Walkers made room for him, then paused to stare after him as he went by.

He couldn't blame them if they were jittery, he supposed. Fort Such had never gone short of publicity in the capital, most of it bad. He figured folks here would be surprised to learn that the vast majority of the sparse population down there in the desert comprised loners and losers and life's pathetic failures who simply liked the easy-going atmosphere of a town without laws. The gunfighter elite, which gave the place its wide notoriety, comprised maybe a baker's dozen, top.

And thought – a baker's dozen less one. Maybe. He had to front the governor first. If Fitzhenry rejected his application for absolution his only option would be to drift back south and figure out what his number two choice might be. Either that or else throw in the towel and drink himself to death as he'd seen many a fast gun do once they passed a certain milestone in their lives.

He shook his head and quickened his stride. 'Can that, Rogan! You made a decision to go for amnesty and you've got to have as good a chance as any. So just get on with it!'

En route to the mansion he found himself cutting across the plaza just as a crowd came spilling from the courthouse, a tall and skinny all-white building with a bell tower and Old Glory fluttering bravely above the pillared entrance way.

He propped.

After a time his would-be drygulchers from the previous night appeared, heavily shackled by both hands and legs and prodded along none too gently by a pair of burly deputies. The accused were greeted by both jeering and cheering, and a deputy slugged a ragged-assed citizen with his baton when he ventured too close.

Rogan kept on.

He'd been reassured that last night's 'welcoming committee' was just a pair of bums with a grudge – he didn't know what about. Nor did he care. The two were merely minnows from the shallows, not the man-eaters he knew he would eventually find lurking someplace if he got to stay on here.

In any case, he accepted as a fact of life that few men anyplace attracted attention as did his notorious breed. That applied to 'gunners', like himself, as well as 'gunslingers', say, like Kip Silver. The distinction was that gunners mostly hired their guns legitimately while a gunslinger would blast anyone if the money was right.

Ten minutes later found him standing across the paved road from the home and official headquarters of the most powerful man in this part of the country.

55

He was impressed again, as he had been before.

The citizenry of Capital City were proud of the governor's mansion, even though precious few of them ever got to see beyond those high iron gates.

It was a large two-storeyed construction fashioned of brick, stone, mortar, timber and adobe mud and was positioned impressively upon the graceful slope of a spruce-covered hill two blocks south of the square. In a city of clapboard, mud bricks and mazes of back alleys, battered squares and evil-smelling cattle marshalling yards, this was a minor castle decorated lavishly with red stone, heavy hewn logs, elegant brick and tile work and boasted a steeply sloped, tiled roof painted gold.

The place was designed to impart a sense of power and permanency to the sprawling hodge-podge of architectural styles comprising this storeyed city of the plains. Built by one of the original cattle barons as a monument to himself, it had already housed three successive governors, two of whom had been dismissed before their time was up. The third and current occupant of the mansion was Abel Fitzhenry, who might or might not get to serve out his full term depending largely on how he acquitted himself in the looming showdown between the entrenched cattlemen and the railroad.

Four sentries in pale blue jackets and black boots stood lined up across the open entrance to the mansion. All snapped smartly alert when the broad-shouldered man with the swinging stride crossed from the opposite side of the wide thoroughfare.

'Halt!' a moustached officer shouted, and Rogan

obligingly stopped and nodded.

'Rogan,' he said. 'I'm expected.'

'We know who you are, sir.'

The officer came forward with clicking heels, rifle held at the port. He appeared to bristle on realizing that up close he was both shorter than the gunfighter and less broad of shoulder. He raked Rogan up and down with hostile eyes, lifted his chin aggressively.

'Your business, sir?'

'You know why I'm here, junior.'

The moment he spoke, Rogan regretted it. But old habits were hard to break. It was instinctive to treat nobodies like this badly. But he knew if he was serious about the decision he'd made last week, and the reason behind his long journey to the capital, then he would have to do better.

'I mean – sir,' he added.

The officer's face was white with anger. For a moment it seemed he might be ready to take this further. Then a sudden change came over him. It was likely that instinct more than intelligence suddenly registered the danger – and the longer he stood there meeting Rogan's flat stare the shakier he got.

He made to speak but had to cough to clear his throat. Rogan gave him a wintry smile of understanding and their little test of strength was over.

'Ahh ... Jackson,' the deflated officer finally croaked to his junior officer. 'Conduct Mr Rogan upstairs and apprise the deputy governor of his presence. Immediately!'

The young man could not suppress a grin of admiration as he escorted the visitor inside and across the vast lobby for the stairs.

'Bet you enjoyed that, eh, Rogan?'

Rogan made no reply. This was a serious moment. He sensed he'd almost wrecked everything when there had been no need to play tough. And wondered, mounting the carpeted stairway, if maybe he'd ridden the blood trails too long after all. That the changes he hoped to achieve here could prove beyond his grasp.

'The hell they will!' he muttered as they gained the landing. 'Quitting Such was the hard part. All you've got to do here is talk straight and curb your tongue, pilgrim!'

He followed the trooper along a broad corridor panelled in oak and was conducted into a waiting-room lined with chairs.

'Governor's aide Tierney will be with you in a moment, Mr Rogan.'

'I've got an appointment with Fitzhenry.'

'Formalities, sir,' the man said apologetically, and was turning to go when the door opened and a slim, hard-faced official appeared.

'Ah, Mr Rogan, I suspect?' Tierney's accent was clipped and precise. He nodded and he swung his door fully open. 'Rade Tierney. After you, Mr Rogan.'

The room was spacious but hardly welcoming. Much like its occupant, Rogan reflected, removing his hat. Already, after just twenty seconds acquaintance, he'd tabbed Rade Tierney as someone over-impressed with himself. Yet he couldn't see why. This business of applying for amnesty was shaping up to be tougher than he'd thought.

Without inviting his visitor to be seated, Tierney resumed his seat and began rapping out a series of questions: date and place of birth, religious beliefs if any, war service, prior employment, political affiliations, etc.

Clay responded monosyllabically. When the question concerning his politics came up he didn't answer at all.

Tierney glanced up sharply. 'Political affiliations or leanings—'

'I heard you. What are yours?'

The man flushed and jumped erect. 'Look here, gunfighter—'

'Don't say something you might live to regret – sonny!'

Instantly Tierney came out from behind his desk and strode for the door.

'Security! Remove this man from my—'

He broke off when Rogan, moving with incredible speed for a man his size, covered two long strides and seized him by a shoulder, fingers digging into the bone. He dragged the man's shocked white face close to his own and lowered his tone to a hiss.

'I'm here to see Fitzhenry and not some upstart shipping clerk, junior. Go tell your security to disappear then you get moving and find Fitzhenry inside one minute or you can tell him our deal is off. You hear me, bus-boy?'

He released his grip and heaved, sending the aide to the governor of Southwest County clear across the hallway to crash into the wall and almost go down.

'Well, what are you waiting for? Move!'

The moment an ashen Tierney vanished clutching a numbed shoulder, Rogan knew it was all over. He'd really believed he could make the change, if he was serious. Now he was brawling with minions who could quite likely knock his prospects into a cocked hat.

Seemed he might have left it too late to change his life after all. Had mixed with the wrong breed too long to change.

And thought bitterly, 'You can take the man out of Fort Such but can't take Fort Such out of the man.'

Jamming his hat on his head he strode from the suite, rounded into the hallway and almost collided with the governor of Southwest County.

He propped and stared blankly. What to say? Plainly there was nothing that would have any effect. He made to step past but slender fingers gripped his bicep.

'Mr Rogan? I've been looking forward to this. Please come—'

'Look, Governor, I just manhandled your flunky and I—'

'Yes, I know. I met Rade on the stairs. He did appear a little distressed. But he is young and will recover. Who knows, it may even improve his disposition.' He appeared to wink as he motioned towards his doorway. 'You've come a long way. Do allow me to offer you a refreshment.'

Rogan blinked. He'd anticipated outrage and possibly rejection before he'd even got halfway started. It took a moment to absorb the fact that the governor appeared anything but angered by the incident. Strange – that was for sure. But he wasn't about to fret any about that. Instead he forced a grin and nodded. Refreshments sounded just fine.

CHAPTER 4

TERROR ON
THE STREETS

The cattlemen were gathered in the lobby when the governor emerged with his visitor. There were three of them and together they comprised the Southwest County Cattle Combine. Urgent and important matters had brought Osgood, Taylor and Quinn to the governor's mansion today. Yet even though their appointment had been made days earlier the ranchers had still been kept waiting over half an hour today. And still no sign of Fitzhenry.

'Upstart son of a bitch!' muttered Big Sam Taylor, chomping on a cud of shag cut. 'Who does he think he is, keeping us hanging on?'

'Yeah . . . who?' supported runty Quinn of the Epic spread which shared common boundaries with Osgood's Double X and Taylor's Cross Trail to the south-west.

Only iron jawed Osgood remained silent, but not without effort. As leader of the cattle triumvirate he wielded real power in Southwest County. He hated the governor, suspected the man of trying to destroy the Cattle Combine, yet today had come determined to hang on to his temper.

This would not be easy, particularly in view of recent developments here at the mansion, where a new and seemingly threatening element had entered into the chequered mosaic of Capital City. Somebody some called a 'gunner'.

They were yet to sight this hardcase, but Rogan had already seen the three arrive to be shown upstairs by what appeared to be a fawning Rade Tierney.

Abruptly Rogan stepped into the light slanting through the west windows. The trio started, recognizing him instantly from the pages of the *Territory Gazette.*

'So . . . it looked like these rumours they'd heard about some Fort Such heller coming north in search of amnesty weren't just tall stories after all!' their expressions seemed to shout.

'Ahh, gentlemen.' Fitzhenry's voice was smooth, almost patronizing as he emerged from his inner sanctum. He'd been locked in combat with the county's cattlemen throughout his tenure here and suddenly sensed this day might have dealt him some kind of unexpected advantage. He gestured towards a motionless Rogan. 'Allow me to introduce Mr—'

'We know who he is,' broke in a red-faced Osgood, Combine chairman and bitter adversary of the

Fitzhenry administration. The big man glared at Rogan, was forced to look up. 'By God, so it's come to this! Not content to try and destroy us with your stinking railroad, now you're cozying up to hired killers and outlaws, Fitzhenry. We heard something about this but didn't believe it. Have you taken leave of your senses, man?'

It was a long speech for a man in the grip of a temper tantrum. Too long to the governor's taste.

'You're Osgood,' Rogan interjected. 'I've seen your picture and met a whole mess of folks who say you've ruined and cheated to get where you are. You seem to talk mighty big for a man this whole county calls a son of a bitch.'

The rancher went white. For a moment it seemed he would actually lash out at the gunfighter. Suddenly the aide and three housemen appeared from no place and and got between them.

The governor tugged down the lapels of his conservative grey houndstooth jacket. His face was set hard. Rogan was surprised by just how tough this ex-general and educated man of affairs appeared in that moment.

'Your appointment is hereby cancelled, Osgood. I have done my best to deal fairly with you people despite the fact that I now know you all to be both dishonest, conniving and habitual liars. I may have been moved to attempt some compromise between you cattlemen and the railroad prior to this, but I shall not have any truck with people who've ruled the roost so long they have grown too arrogant to distinguish between compromise and blatant defiance of the law and its structures.'

He swung on his aide.

'Mr Tierney, see the gentlemen off the premises and inform security they are to be denied admission hereafter.'

Sharp-featured Tierney appeared to pale. 'Governor, are you sure that—?'

'You're not procrastinating, are you, sir?' Fitzhenry said warningly.

'Goddamnit!' the choleric Osgood yelled, flailing his arms. 'I don't care if you're the governor or Davy Crockett, you can't—'

He broke off, realizing the gunfighter had suddenly stepped so close they were almost touching.

'You should know the governor's just agreed to accept my application for amnesty, cattleman. And once I'm sworn in I'll hold a rank equal to a deputy sheriff in this town. So, knowing that, maybe it might be safer all round if you people just accept the fact that you're not wanted, and vamoose?'

It was an education to watch a powerful man with authority extending over an entire region, appear to crumble before this challenge. Osgood took two backwards steps. He clutched at his chest and coughed. He could not believe it was happening. But the firm hand of the governor's assistant on his elbow convinced him.

'Come along, Mr Osgood,' said Tierney, shooting a withering stare at his superior, who wore a half-smile. He was forced to clear his dry throat. 'All you gentlemen, come along. I'll attempt to secure you an appointment with the governor at another more convenient time.'

'But don't hold your breath,' Fitzhenry called after the party as they were guided for the stairs.

Rogan felt like a smoke. He felt tense, yet positive. Although widely experienced in the violent ways of the South-West, he had never pictured himself playing a role in a matter of obvious importance under the roof of the most powerful man in the entire territory.

Fitzhenry stepped out on to a small balcony to watch his visitors clamber into their rigs below. Rogan joined him.

'Does our agreement still stand?' he wanted to know.

The governor swung to face him.

'It certainly does, Rogan. In fact I'd go so far as to say that this little drama merely confirms my original assessment of you as a potential asset to my administration. In the area of law enforcement, of course.'

Relieved, he nodded and turned to go.

'Ahh, one last thing, Rogan. What transpired just now. Those cattlemen won't forget this. I have never been able to bring them to book on any serious charge even when I've been certain they have been up to their necks in rustling, intimidation, even perhaps far graver crimes. I am impressed with how you handled things, but be warned, sir. While assisting the government to establish and enforce real law and order, it will be your responsibility for the time being, to be both watchful and careful at all times, particularly after this little set-to. If the Cattle Combine fails to prevent the completion of the railroad – which will throw open the entire cattle market of the territory for free trade and so destroy their monopoly – they could face ruin and may well turn on their enemies, of which you are now one. Do you understand?'

He nodded and went down the stairs. He couldn't recall a brighter afternoon.

Kip Silver's fat grey mare moved lightly over the trampled grass that had been flattened by cattle then burned white by the sun of late summer.

He whistled tunelessly as he saw the huddled mud houses move slowly by. This was one of the oldest sectors of the county and he believed some of these huts had stood here for hundreds of years on the banks of a dismal grey river that never boasted a decent flow yet which never ran totally dry.

He sneered, untouched by the plight of people who lived this way, like dumb beasts. As untouched as he was by the imminent fate of the man he'd come to kill.

Jackman was his name. All he knew was that he was a trigger man of some breed who'd shot and killed a rich merchant in a drunken argument over a woman. She would have been some strumpet, was his guess. But then he admitted to holding a low opinion of women in general. That had to do with the fact that few females ever took a shine to the man who now alone wore the uncontested mantle of gun king of Fort Such. Occasionally he struck a girl who was fascinated by the legend surrounding him and was perversely drawn by the thrill of making love to a man who had sent so many to their graves.

This did not happen very often. He knew he was handsome, feared and famous but had long since accepted the fact that he scared the hell out of far more females than he appealed to.

His sudden bitter laugh sounded in the high afternoon air, causing a goat tethered to a gatepost to prick its ears.

He looked at the sun and decided to get it over and done with sooner than later. He kicked his mount with both heels causing the fat mare to grunt in protest before breaking into a trot.

It was two hours later when he rode into Five Hollows just as the sun was settling upon the western rim.

A ragged-assed urchin sighted him and ran, disappearing like a rat down a drainpipe.

'Smart kid,' he mused, and steered Mirabelle towards the saloon.

It was almost too easy, he reflected later. The fat man who'd cheated his ranch partner out of a lousy five hundred bucks on a stock deal a week earlier had been drinking at the Star and Hammer ever since. He was celebrating his triumph and frequently took out his fat roll of notes both to count them and also to make sure everyone realized what an up-and-coming rangeland tycoon he was.

He cried when the total stranger with the silver-blond hair and fastidiously neat trail rig calmly offered him the option. He could die standing, or else could get down on his knees and pray for mercy, and still die anyway.

In the end he'd attempted to draw his rusty old shooter and died with one bullet in the heart.

Nobody from the ashen saloonkeeper to his fear-frozen clientele could understand why the sleek killer, after fingering a fresh bullet into his Colt, sauntered across to the corpse and kicked it before mounting up and riding off.

Kip Silver never did anything without a reason. His spite tonight stemmed from the fact that the contract killing had not given him the customary kick of plea-sure he expected.

That was enough to sour the whole thing for him. As a result, he was soon taking pot shots at those huddled little mud dwellings he passed on his way back for the main trail that would take him back to the Fort.

By the time a bloated yellow moon was riding the night sky he was able to identify just why his mood was so dark and why he seemed to have this bitter taste continually in his mouth.

The latest issue of the *Capital Star* newspaper was responsible. Yesterday, on his way here, he'd gotten to read that rag, was sneering and smirking his way through it when he came upon the brief article under the headline that announced:

RAILROAD GIVEN GO-AHEAD!

He could care less about railroads or the million-aires who seemed to be stringing the high iron just about anyplace where God had land these days. But the *Capital City Star* seemed genuinely excited about the fact that, following long delays due to opposition from the local cattlemen, the governor had finally granted the half-finished Larribee to Capital City Line permission to complete the final twenty miles of track connecting both cities. When operational, this would cut transport time for stock from the region to the cattle markets up at Quintlock from five weeks by hoof to just one day by rail.

'So?' he'd sneered aloud. 'Who cares?'

He had been about to toss the rag aside when a name in the final paragraph caught his eye. Clay Rogan. Naturally he'd read on to learn the governor himself had given Rogan some credit for this 'great event' owing to the big role he'd played in curbing Capital City's cattle barons. These men were accused by the paper of having monopolized the region's cattle industry by force and scaring off all competition over many years.

Staring bleakly at the trail stretching ahead in the moonlight now, Silver knew he should just let it rest. So, what if big Rogan had deserted his own kind? And if he had licked the boots of the governor and swallowed his amnesty pill like a good little boy? Did anyone really care if he now worked as some kind of gunner-lawman who just days ago had kicked Bad Abe Walsh out of the city with orders to return to Fort Such and stay there?

And knew he cared all the way down to his fancy boots.

The very fact that Rogan quit the game and came seeking salvation from their enemies in Capital City, was in itself an act of treason in the killer's eyes.

But actually to sign on with the lawdogs and turn against his own like a mongrel dog?

Was there a name for anybody that low?

The gunman absently fingered the beautiful inlaid butt of his .45 and stared up at the moon with blood in his eye, a look that surely boded ill for somebody.

Without warning, he kicked the fat mare hard and heeled her into a run. Suddenly he needed to reach Fort Such fast.

The governor's wife stepped past a Pueblo smoking a corn-husk cigarette upon the steps of the corner store.

It was mid-morning in Capital City and she had not slept since the previous night, and then only fitfully.

Of course, she realized people said she was crazy. The governor's wife spent hours daily, either in Poortown, or at the uptown hospice she'd created for the poor and sick called the Centre, instead of flitting about the mansion in silks and crinolines and flirting with visiting dignitaries. What sort of abnormal behaviour was this for a mature woman?

In reflective moments like this she sometimes wondered if maybe they might not be right.

She was overdue at the Centre yet deliberately headed in the opposite direction today. There were times when even a woman dedicated to her charity work could feel she had seen one battered wife or one knife-gashed limb too many, and this bright morning seemed to be one.

She considered the city looked its best today, although many might query use of the word 'best'. Some saw the capital as squalid degenerating to impossible. She'd never been one of these. She might concede it was old, poverty-stricken and often over-violent, but she could also see the more positive side.

Her head filled with smells as she entered the square – animals, people, liquor, cooking meat, beans, cheap wine, tortillas and sweating Indians. And mingling with all these by now familiar odours were the sounds of laughter, cursing, braying, neighing, barking and thrumming guitars, all blending in with the one eternal sound of the square – vendors shouting their wares.

She was always amazed by the number of people who knew her and called her by name now. Some might think her strange and odd, deserting the luxury of the governor's mansion to spend so much of her time, even often sleeping over at the Centre which was nothing more than a vast abandoned hide shed recently converted into a haven for the sick and poor by people just like the governor's lady.

She was halfway past the American House Hotel when she stopped on impulse and went inside. There was a welcoming buffet and coffee room to one side of the desk, where the clerk grinned and gave her a cheery *Buenos dias, señora*, as she went by.

On making this decision to enter the hotel, she was well aware that Carrie Morelos frequently stopped off here mornings on her way somewhere or other, and was delighted to find the young woman seated by the big windows overlooking the square now.

They greeted one another affectionately. Carrie, young, lithe and startlingly pretty, was the daughter of a genuine rarity in the capital these times, a wealthy Mexican. Carrie, spirited rebel who nonetheless often put in long hours at the Centre, was plainly happy to see the governor's wife, and, naturally, was full of questions.

What was this awful gunman really like? Was the governor honestly intending to grant him amnesty? Had she seen him, and was he as terrible as he sounded?

Isabel Fitzhenry lifted both hands palms forward, and laughed.

'Please, please . . . if you're talking about the man from Fort Such, Carrie, I haven't even sighted him. But why all this curiosity concerning just another gunman in our lives?'

'Well, I suppose it's because he sounds so different and, well, interesting. Honestly, Isabel, the men in this place! They are either drunkards, lechers, wheeler-dealers – or cowboys or railroad workers brawling with one another with hardly the time to glance at a woman. You must admit this Rogan fellow sounds different.'

Isabel sobered.

'I stopped by at the mansion last evening. All Abel wanted to do was talk about this man. I couldn't believe he's already had him signed on as some kind of special deputy. I mean, what is this place coming to? One would imagine we have all the trouble and violence we need, what with the railroad and the cattlemen at loggerheads and the usual level of violence on the streets. But no, my 'visionary' spouse takes a liking to this person and honestly seems to believe he might help settle things down and promote the cause of law and order. Perhaps you can understand now why I spend most of my time at the Centre?'

'Speaking of which, Isabel,' the younger woman said, checking the fob watch pinned to her jacket lapel. 'Didn't you tell me the doctor is coming to the Centre at ten today?'

'Oh, my goodness, it completely slipped my mind,' the older woman cried, rising quickly. She squeezed the girl's hands on the table. 'Might you be along later, dear?'

The other smiled wryly. 'Unless I meet the man of my dreams and run away to California to live in sin – fat chance! But yes, I suppose I will stop by.'

They blew one another kisses as the governor's wife went out through the doors, leaving her young companion staring upon the plaza.

Carrie Morelos was beautiful, cynical, spoiled and rebellious. She was aware of this for her many critics told her so often enough. They hoped that by so doing she might get to moderate her behaviour and start acting like the educated, well-bred daughter of an important citizen should.

In her rare moments of sober self-analysis the girl seriously doubted this transformation would ever take place. There was much about life that offended and exasperated her, and she was always looking for new ideas, wider visions and, above all, changes for the better.

For a long time now she had been burdened by a strengthening feeling that, if she were really genuine about all these high-minded changes she advocated, she might be better off living somewhere else – anywhere else but Capital City, Southwest County, USA.

Impetuous as always, she suddenly rose, signalled to the woman to put her check on her father's account. She then went outside where life as it was actually lived here – not in her mind – surged by just like always.

She had brought her driver along today. The man signalled from the spring buggy parked close by. She sighed dramatically as she crossed to the hitchrail and climbed in.

'Where to, *señorita*?'

'The nearest drug den, thank you, Alfonse.'

'*Señorita*?'

'Just being silly, Alfonse. You might as well take me to Poortown and the Centre.'

The driver wheeled the rig expertly through the crowds and his passenger was leaning back against leather cushions when her eye was drawn by a tall figure standing on the walk before the large impressive new offices of the Great Southwest Railroad.

She frowned faintly as the gap narrowed. She had never seen this one before. He was tall and broad, obviously American and quite intimidating looking, she thought. She noted that walkers stepped around him, some staring back as they passed. She saw a man stare, turn to spit, move on. The stranger glanced after him, then was about to step down when he realized her rig was approaching.

He halted and for a moment their glances met, his expressionless, hers less so. For in that moment, the rich man's daughter sensed rather than knew, that this must be the newcomer she and the governor's wife had just been discussing. She'd heard he was tall, and assumed he would also appear formidable. Her quick eye had not missed the big gun strapped low on his right thigh, gunfighter style.

What was the name. . . ? Rogan, that was it. And glancing back through the mica window to see him staring after the gig with no change of expression, felt her heart sink. Like Isabel and many like her, Carrie Morelos was sick to death of the violence and poverty, the plague of lawlessness and uncertainty here. So many here craved change. But what did they get?

Another gunman – this time simply a bigger one! Surely the insane were running the asylum!

Earlier she had simply been attempting to shock her friend Isabel when threatening to run off with a cheap gambler who would probably beat her. Just for that bitter moment, however, it did not seem such a foolish idea.

Clay Rogan sat in the sun on the front porch of his hotel. The cigar he smoked was Cuban, the pistol riding his right hip was American, the angry young man standing in the dust by the hitchrail cursing him, Mexican born.

Rogan calmly reached into a pocket. His fingers

found a coin. He took it out and flipped it to his one-man 'Gunfighter Go Home!' squad.

The man caught the coin with dexterity, was about to start in cursing again when he glanced at it and realized it was a ten-dollar gold piece.

'Madonna!' he gasped, almost completely sobering. A drunken tear sprang to the eye and he was about to recant and offer his apologies when Rogan's lips barely moved: 'Take it and get before I break both your legs!'

'Dirty gringo!' he managed to get out. But his heart was not in it and with a final obscene gesture, he spun and was gone, bare feet flashing whitely.

Still a picture of relaxation, Rogan blew a cloud of smoke into the square and returned to watching Capital City in the afternoon.

Strangely, Mission Square seemed almost peaceful despite the tension building by the hour. Occasionally, cowboys from the Cattle Combine would ride by on their big flash horses, sixshooters sagging from holsters, cigarettes pasted to bottom lips and blood in their eyes when they saw him lounging there like he thought he was somebody important.

It might have been the balmy sunshine or simply the shocked disbelief at the news that the railroad had returned to full-scale track-laying overnight, but nobody seemed able to work up a genuine sense of outrage right then, other than the one luckless bum the gunfighter had just bought off with a ten-dollar gold piece.

Not that Rogan was complaining about the lull.

Capital City could stay this quiet for as long as it liked as far as he was concerned. But he knew that would not happen. The governor, the very man who craved peace most, had touched the flame to the tinder with his decision favouring the railroad, had warned his new security marshal that something would surely 'blow' as a result, the only uncertainty being when.

But the gunfighter was skilled at making the most of any patch of peace that might happen by, knowing as sure as God made green apples that it could not last, would not ... and who was this handsome woman approaching along the plankwalk anyway?

She paused, seemed about to continue on, then pursed her lips and turned back to face his faintly curious gaze.

'I've already told my husband I do not approve of you, Mr Rogan,' she declared in a nicely cultivated tone. She peered at him intently as he leaned forward. 'For some reason I just now felt it important that you should hear that from my own lips.'

He doffed his hat and flicked ash from his cheroot.

'It always helps to know who's for you and who's against in my line of work, Mrs Fitzhenry.'

'I suspect you're mocking me?'

'Not at all. But in my own defence I must point out that from experience gleaned in towns like the capital, and in times like you're having here, I've figured it most always is better having someone like me on your side of the fence than the opposite.'

She gave that some thought. Then, 'I must say you

don't seem exactly as I expected. Tell me, are you married, Mr Rogan?'

'Still searching, ma'am, still searching.'

'And still mocking me. Well, I suppose I deserve it – er, why are you rising, sir?'

'Why, to escort you wherever you happen to be going, ma'am.' He placed a hand upon her arm and turned sober. 'Not joking, Mrs Fitzhenry. Everything might appear calm and placid right now but I can tell you Capital City is a million miles away from that. Trouble's brewing. And I *am* here to protect folks even if you might think different. Shall we go?'

'I can assure you I'm safer on this square with all the people that know me and—' she began, then broke off, studying him. 'Well, if you insist, young man . . . I am on my way to the Centre. . . .'

He did insist. Which was how he came to be introduced formally to the most striking young woman he'd seen in years when Carrie Morelos showed up just minutes after they'd reached the big old converted hide shed on Holt Street.

For the first time that day Rogan found himself able to quit thinking about the tensions gripping the city. But before he could get to pay her even one half-compliment, Miss Morelos asked, with pretty lips pursed, if he might possibly refrain from maiming or killing anyone that day as their emergency beds were all filled.

It was a sober and wiser Rogan who bade both ladies a grave goodbye and headed back to what he did best. But before he could reach the square, it happened. From out of a side street erupted a sudden rattle of drums and the thud of marching feet. As he propped, a column of marchers with cowboy hats and naked six-guns in their hands came swinging into sight, roaring at the tops of their voices:

We're gonna hang all the railroaders
    To a sour apple tree,
Yes we are,
    Oh yes were are – yeehahhh!

The human flood kept coming, a woman screamed in terror and a six-gun roared even before Rogan could haul his Colt .45.

CHAPTER 5

RIVER OF BLOOD

The big trouble had begun fomenting just an hour earlier within the oak-pannelled walls of the Cattlemen's Club.

The meeting went into its third hour. Outside, gun-hung cowboys from the three spreads were yawning and scratching and staring resentfully at the closed and guarded double doors.

The scatter of cigarette butts revealed to passers-by just how long they'd been there and how tense and tedious it all must be. The ranch hands were simple men of action who couldn't understand why the Double X, Cross Trail and Epic bosses weren't simply doing what they had done successfully so often in the past. Which was – if someone was giving you serious trouble, anytime, anyplace – send in the boys!

It had worked before. What was so different now?

The very fact that they thought along those lines explained why they were forty-bucks-a-month cowhands while their employers smoked five-dollar cigars and holidayed in San Francisco once a year.

Admittedly Osgood from the Double X, fat, red-faced and arrogant, had initially floated the notion of attacking the railroad headquarters immediately following the County Court's landmark decision to award the line permission to complete its last stretch of track from Larribee. Yet he had been howled down by the remaining two-thirds of the triumvirate.

Because he liked to sulk – and feeling he'd seldom had better reason to do so – Osgood had contributed little to the wordy marathon from that point onwards. This bothered his partners not at all. Taylor and Quinn were hard-nosed realists and as such kept proposing and rejecting plan after plan to circumvent the county government but finally were beginning to run out of ideas by this.

Quinn was first to slump back into his chair and wearily signal to the waiter for a drink.

'What riles me – really riles me right now – is that when we first blocked off the spur up at Larribee by blowing up their lousy bridge, the government was off busy with the Indians.' He slugged down half his drink and belched. 'We could have gone on and put the torch to the whole damned work site and likely gotten rid of them for keeps with minimum risk .Why didn't we do that?'

'None of us had a hankering to do ten years' hard in Yuma, is why!' Hawk-featured Quinn wasn't pulling any punches now. For years, the trio had ruled the rangelands, had made their fortunes by squeezing out rivals, manipulating the industry,

82

buying rustled stock for a song and selling them for top dollar under their own aegis.

In short, these were all big, illegal operations. But it had kept them in power and dollars with no challengers – until the advent of the railroad.

The main line was building to Quintville in the north when some smart executive took a careful look at the power situation in Capital City and quickly saw the way the big three had the whole cattle industry all locked up tight. The Combine had converted itself into the only market for the dozens of smaller ranchers, whom it paid peanuts. But there was no opportunity to sell elsewhere. This was because the Combine's gunmen-cowboys attacked them every time they attempted to drive, which meant they didn't drive any more. They sold their cattle to the Combine, the Combine drove them to Larribee and pocketed the eighty per cent of the sale price.

Violent things had happened to anyone who tried to alter this situation in the past.

But the railroad executive quickly realized a branch line strung directly overland to Capital City would afford all ranchers in the region the opportunity to sell their product at market price while avoiding the long dangerous drive overland to Larribee where they could be picked off by rustlers, wild Indians – or Combine guns.

Up until the previous week the Combine believed their bribing of government officials would continue to keep them safe from any possible 'invasion by rail'. But there had been a major clean-out in official circles recently and when the matter was again put to the vote the presiding chairman not only agreed the ban should be lifted but insisted upon it. That achieved, he approved the construction of the spur line from Larribee to Capital City the very same day.

Following a long thick silence, Osgood finally came out of his sulk and framed the big question; 'Does this mean we're done for? We've let ourselves grow so reliant on buying up the small spreads' stock for chicken feed and on-selling to the Larribee abbattoirs for big bucks, we scarce raise any stock worth a damn now ourselves.'

'We've faced problems before,' growled Taylor. 'But we never had the railroad slinging steel in our direction before. But there's got to be a way of dealing with this. What do you say, Quinn?'

'What I say,' Quinn said tightly, 'is that I'm quitting!'

The two stared uncomprehendingly.

'What, tough-talking Quinny throwing in his hand?' Osgood sounded shocked. 'You're just going to let the railroad reach out and gobble up all we've—'

'Not quit the battle, you fool!' Quinn was on his feet and his face was hard as stone. 'I'm saying I'm gonna quit the Combine, damn you!'

Osgood and Taylor were not sure they had heard right. Quit the Combine? After ten years of crime and high profits? And Quinn – supposedly the toughest operator of the trio?

'Well, I sure as shooting never expected to see the day when you'd buckle up and play yellow dog—' Taylor said bitterly. But Quinn cut him off.

'What I'm trying to say, if you clean out your ears, is that I'll quit the Combine if it throws in the towel. Not quit the fight. I'll continue on my own – just me against the railroad. I might well lose out but by Judas I'll go down with all guns blazing.' He shook a clenched fist. 'They'll only ever get to suck up our market – yours and mine – over my dead body. So if you weak sisters have got nothing else to say, get the hell out and leave me to run the Cattlemen's Club and this here battle my way!'

It was silent for a long minute as Osgood and Taylor digested this outburst. They analysed it until the hard logic in the third man's words hit home like a double jolt of Kentucky bourbon.

Moments later all three were shaking hands and punching the air. Suddenly Osgood and Taylor realized that all that had been needed from the outset of the current crisis had been for someone to get up on his hind legs and remind them they were still kings of the county and could go on being so providing they simply quit acting like old women and got back to what they did best – fighting and winning.

For had not the Combine always won?

They quickly got down to figuring exactly how and by what means they would go about reminding this government-bluffed county of that vital fact of life.

It was not all that long before hard-jawed Mike Quinn came up with *another* big idea. He first convinced his partners they had no option but to strike fast and with full strength to bring the track-laying to an end, then reinforced his reputation as the mastermind of the Combine by identifying not

85

only where they must strike for maximum effect, but also how and when.

Quinn did not call for a vote as was the custom. This crisis posed the greatest threat the Combine had ever faced and the turmoil had shaken the old structure of power to its foundations. It no longer comprised three members of equal status and strength. Quinn had emerged as by far the strongest and most clear-headed. If they survived – as they were beginning to believe they would now – it would be all due to Quinn.

He continued to speak and his foot soldiers listened attentively.

The brawl was in full cry when the deputy came charging through the batwings, swinging his billy club.

'All right, you damned drunks!' he shouted. 'Back up against the bar, and you, Billy Zeke – you get rid of that bottle, hear?'

Ugly Billy Zeke heard but was far too drunk to take orders. He worked for the railroad, and it had been a bunch of Combine riders that had jumped him and his pard for no special reason here, touching off a ruckus that quickly got out of hand.

The brawler hurled his bottle in the general direction of the law then went down on both knees a split second later when a king hit caught him under the left ear.

He collapsed, down and out. When he came around he was dazed to find himself being cheered to the echo by a saloon full of railroad workers, contractors and security guns, along with two score labourers, gandy dancers and grade-layers with muscles on their breath.

It was not until after peace was fully restored and his head stopped aching that Billy Zeke learned the brawl had in fact been quelled by none other than their new special marshal along with Sheriff Tom Doherty, who'd done what they came to do then moved on.

'But . . . but I thought the law was agin' the railroad, boys,' he said. 'How come. . . ?'

'Don't strain your brain, boy,' a cowboy advised, holding a cold compress to a badly blackened eye. 'This here town is standing on its ear and nobody seems to know who's playing the fiddle or who's collecting the poor man's pennies any more.'

The waddy's puzzlement was understandable for this was surely a night of uncertainty and alarms in which everybody seemed to sense there might well be some kind of major explosion between cattlemen and the rejuvenated railroad before sunrise.

This taut atmosphere was exacerbated by the fact that nobody seemed sure what side the major powers such as government, law office, the railroad and the cattlemen would fall on should things run out of control.

The town scarcely believed it when daybreak came without another single major incident. And sipping a weak whisky with the governor at the mansion as a red sun loomed over the horizon, Clay Rogan was as puzzled and relieved as anybody.

Yet experience warned that whatever kind of crisis

everyone anticipated had only been postponed, not averted.

Even so, he was content to stand at the big bay windows drinking coffee, as he mused, 'This could almost be a decent place if a man could get rid of the riff-raff. . . .' And smiled humourlessly at the next thought that sprang from that. In his exhaustion, he supposed he'd just described hell.

This 'gunslinger-turned-peacemaker', as the editor of the newspaper had described him in an edgy recent article, plainly needed to lay his head down and get in maybe twelve hours' sleep.

But first, he would take one last turn round a town which, for some loco reason, he seemed to be getting to feel more and more responsible for.

Surely that couldn't be healthy?

On the sawdust covered floor of a tin-roofed saloon lay a dead man. A lone rider hammered away through the vast black cavern of the night. The air was mild but Kip Silver felt almost a chill as he glanced back over his shoulder.

No sign of pursuing riders – but he knew they were there.

Behind him was death, ahead the unmarked trail leading back to Fort Such . . . twenty miles distant.

The fat mare was not going to make it. He'd pushed hard all day to reach one-horse Midas, where he'd planned to overnight and spell the mare for maybe a solid twelve hours.

How was he to know some rich rancher's big-mouth son would get a skinful and start in on him after finding out who he was?

He'd been patient, he told himself. Had warned the tall fool not to mess with him. But a man could only take so much, and when Laddy Big Bucks boozily accused him of shooting some distant kinsman he'd never even heard of, then sent somebody to fetch Midas's hard-nosed sheriff, the fool was 'just rushing towards death'.

That was how an ancient Fort Such sage had once described men like that, he reflected bitterly, as he ducked his head beneath a sweeping branch and cursed when it almost swept his hat away. They talked too much, never had the sense to size up genuine danger when it crossed their path, were brought up to believe that money and power bestowed upon them some kind of immunity.

He'd said quietly – hanging on to his always unpredictable temper, 'Just walk away while you still can, junior. Nobody will think any the worse of you here.' But then he'd just had to add, 'Even a thumb-sucking mamma's boy like yourself would have to know you wouldn't stand the chance of a snowball in hell against me – drunk or sober. Ask anybody. Go on, do yourself a big favour and ask—'

That was as far as he got. The heir to twenty thousand acres of prime grassland and all that grazed upon it, grabbed his shooter with passable speed and couldn't believe it when three .45 calibre soft-nosed bullets stitched across his chest and knocked him ten feet across that crummy little bar-room before his legs collapsed under him.

That one-horser *would* boast a famous name

badgeman and two deputies, he mused cynically, as the silver trace of the river finally showed up ahead – and hoofbeats thudded closer behind.

Clint Stormer was his name. And right now he would surely be thinking just how fine it would look blazoned across the newspapers of the territory, the headline news that he, Sheriff Clint Stormer, had finally put paid to the life and times of Kip Silver, *desperado* and fast gun.

'Dream on, Stormer,' he muttered aloud. And the fat pretty mare pricked her ears at the sound of his voice just as her pace began to falter alarmingly crossing the long-grass plain leading to the river.

He could whip her but he wouldn't do it. He glanced back again . . . and there they were, five dark centaur shapes of horses with riders . . . travelling swifter than bad news.

He turned ahead and flexed his shoulders as he made calculations involving distance, horse speed, the dubious sanctuary of that grey wooded hillside beyond the river.

He started sharply.

Something had whispered past, high overhead. Moments later he heard the sullen whiplash crack of the rifle.

They'd drawn within range yet the river was still a good mile ahead!

Silver glimpsed a spurt of hot orange split the gloom. Another bullet whined past, well off to his right. A third whispered somewhat closer. He calculated the distance at five hundred yards. A hit would be a fluke, but a fluke shot could kill a man just as dead.

The anger kicked in then. Anger exacerbated by affronted pride. Those bastards knew who he was, yet were howling and hooting after him like he was some ragged-assed bum they were chasing for half-hinching a turnip just to keep himself from starving!

He deliberately let the anger build, encouraged it. The mare grunted when he touched heels to her sides gently, yet lifted her gait. The river loomed and they'd stopped shooting, plainly intent on running him down before he reached it.

As they might.

The realization sobered him. But only for a moment.

'Come on, old girl,' he whispered in the failing horse's ear. 'I promise, if we get across I won't ask you to run one more yard. You know I never lie, don't you, sweetheart?'

The animal responded and they reached the river bank with renewed gunfire churning from behind. The mare made it down the steep bank and, at his urgent command, took to the water.

They were yelling behind and when he hipped around in the saddle with water up to his waist, he glimpsed a man astride a white horse closing in fast.

He raised his Colt and squeezed trigger gently. A shriek as high as a woman's voice split the night and the dead-meat thud of the body pitching to earth carried to him clearly – the bastards were that close!

The crossing was a nightmare after he'd looped his gunbelt over the horse's head then slid from the saddle into the cold waters and alternately swam and dived, with leaden death pocking the river all around.

Yet it proved much faster than he might have hoped, and the riders were still milling and shooting from the far bank as he seized hold of the mare's tail and allowed her to drag him onto the grassy bank beneath a big old tree that offered immediate protection.

Shivering and cursing, Silver slapped the animal's rump to set her climbing the bank. He jerked out his Colt and looped the rig over one shoulder as he got behind the tree just as a solitary horseman pushed his mount into the water with a splash.

He knew who that would have to be before he even looked. It could only be Stormer, he of the reputation.

Suppressing the heaving of his chest by an act of will, the killer rested his sixshooter and both supporting hands in the fork of the big old tree and drew a bead on the swimming shapes. The sheriff-guntipper was holding his Winchester up to keep it dry. He was tall and wide-shouldered and was urging the horse on. Slowly, deliberately, Silver drew a bead on that broad chest. He cocked the .45 and closed one eye. Expelling the last breath from his lungs, he waited another moment, then fired.

Dramatically, the lawman rose to stand in his stirrup irons, his rifle spilling on one side of the horse, his hat to the other. He curved backwards without a cry and vanished beneath the grey waves and never reappeared.

Instantly the far riverside erupted into a racketing

of angry gunfire and Kip Silver felt the bullets thudding into the sturdy trunk against which he pressed his back as he sat staring up at the small outline of the mare a hundred feet higher up, his chest heaving to soundless laughter.

Only when he was rested and ready did he stand and begin to climb. He kept the ancient river monarch and her sweeping branches between himself and the survivors, none of whom had dared come anywhere near the water after watching the sheriff's riderless horse struggle back to dry land.

He rested a half hour then swung up and headed north-by-north-west, the faint trail to Capital City stretching away into invisibility between the fat mare's ears.

CHAPTER 6

THE HIGH IRON

Smoke rose in billowing clouds above the work site and swirled about the stocky figure of the works boss standing on the bluff with hands locked behind his back as he watched the 'miracle' continue to unfold below.

Wide-eyed westerners had called it that when they saw the railroad's full work crew in action for the first time. But out here on Choctaw Creek some ten miles due west of Capital City, the whole bustling and amazingly modern operation was now simply and familiarly known as 'the track-layer'. Comprising a large number of mostly coolie labourers, a bunch of yelling and cursing overseers and several huge pieces of machinery, and orchestrated by any amount of cussing and whistling, belching steam and seemingly endless energy, the track-layer operated from before dawn and continued frenetically well into the night, day after day.

Onward they came.

A light car drawn by a runty black horse was driven to the front drawing a sled-car laden with a load of steel rails. Two men waited to seize the front end of the first rail and started forward with it, while others moved in quickly behind to grab hold of the rail every three or four feet of its length and take their share of the load. Once the full length was clear of the car, the men broke into a trot, the coolies chanting some kind of alien rhythm to ensure that all kept in step with their burden.

When the ganger bawled 'Right!' the rail was dropped into place upon the newly laid ties where other workers swarmed to bolt it down, while the coolies trotted back up-track to the car to grab down yet another length of shimmering steel.

The moment one car was emptied it was tipped over on to the sloped side of the track to allow the next car load to come on through, then was muscled back up on to the line and manhandled back to the supply depot to load up once more.

While all the time the air rang to the clamour of steel hammers driving in the spikes to hold the new iron in place, and the overseer lighted his pipe and checked out his fob watch to make doubly sure the operation was maintained at optimum speed.

Prior to this ten days of frantic activity the construction of the spur line from Larribee to Capital City had been delayed for weeks while the cattlemen and the railroad tycoons slugged it out both at the courthouse and in a dozen pitched battles, some of which had even overflowed bloodily into Capital City itself at times.

The governor's decision to permit construction to resume of the vital twenty miles of spur line from Larribee to Capital City had taken the railroad bosses by surprise. But they had quickly recovered and soon had their crews working around the clock, despite apprehension at the possibility that Combine pressure might yet force Fitzhenry to change his mind again and shut them down once more.

At every vantage point above this frenzied scene of endless activity, hard-faced men with rifles paced slowly to and fro – just in case.

Some of these claimed to enjoy the ongoing peace and quiet up there upon the high banks, while others half-wished some trouble might erupt just to ease the tension which sprang from not really knowing if the Combine had actually given up the battle, or were just lulling everyone here into a sense of false security before they struck again.

It was a strange fact of life that, in the capital just a few miles east by this, only a minority seemed interested in all this feverish activity which in time could mean so much to the region's future security and prosperity.

There was good reason for this seeming detachment. Of course, Capital City realized the importance of completing the spur line, and would surely welcome this new age of technology when the first snorting loco wheeled into the soon-to-be completed depot just off the main square.

But the thing that preoccupied the capital man in the street far more than the rail-building itself, was the very real possibility that railroad-Combine hostility might engulf the city itself, and there was not a man, woman or child who was unaware of how savage and bloody that could prove to be.

As a consequence, the entire city was far more preoccupied in trying to decipher whatever the Cattle Combine might be thinking, plotting or planning, rather than in the actual rail-building operation itself.

Tension ruled the county capital in those early days of autumn and the lights in the governor's mansion seemed to burn later and later every night.

Clay Rogan glanced around to ensure there were no other beggars apart from that one-eyed derelict squatting on the front porch of the sheriff's office, before reaching into his hip pocket. A big risk associated with responding to a panhandler in this man's town was that if you were observed you might attract another dozen of the same in a twinkling of an eye.

He tossed a handful of coins to the fellow, who scooped them up with magical dexterity then bestowed a blessing in Spanish.

'Don't be here when I come out, Ramon,' Rogan said, stepping inside. 'The governor wants the city cleaned up for when the railroad comes, *compre*?'

'The saints be with you, *patron*,' the man replied with faked sincerity. Yet as he rose and started off for the shadow, he muttered, 'I hear the whisper, Señor Rogan. . . .'

Rogan halted in the jailhouse doorway. 'What?'

'You should beware.'

'What of?'

'The world is filled with evil . . . even the great mansion itself. . . .'

'Meaning?'

But the man was already gone, limping away to be swallowed by the gloom of the alley so swiftly that it raised doubts concerning just how incapacitated he might really be.

Yet because he had come to half-trust the fellow over time, Rogan found himself considering the warning as he entered the jailhouse's front office to find the sheriff seated with his boots up on the desk blotter, fingers and thumbs pressing the corners of his eyes.

'Ahh, Clay,' Doherty said wearily. 'You caught me loafing – again.'

Rogan had come to know the lawman as anything but lazy. Indeed, in his comparatively short time here he'd been quick to separate the wheat from the chaff just about every place, from the governor's mansion down to the noisome slums of Storytown. He both trusted and liked lean Tom Doherty, a man burdened by one of the toughest jobs in the territory.

Removing his hat and running fingers through his thick dark hair, he considered that thought a minute. He'd come here in search of amnesty while still packing a gun. He'd gotten what he wanted yet the gun never left his side. Would you call that success? Or was it just the same old thing, only under a different label?

Deciding this was no time to be pondering such weighty matters he rested his arm upon the edge of the desk and told the lawman the reason behind his late night call.

It was the rumours . . . again.

Capital City was alive with gossip, lies and half-truths even at normal times, and these were anything but that. The specific rumours he was concerned with tonight were those surrounding the deputy governor. He'd started off badly with Rade Tierney and things had not improved since. He scented something dangerous about the man that made him uneasy. He had picked up a rumour just that day claiming that the deputy governor had been sighted in the company of Combine boss Mike Quinn late at night over in a low-class sector of Poortown.

'Could mean nothing or everything, I guess,' the peace officer muttered after hearing him out. The lawman was genuinely exhausted. Dropping his boots to the floor he opened a drawer and produced a flask. He held it up to Rogan, who shook his head. The man took a swallow, then grimaced. 'That's better, but still not wonderful. I guess I'm plain burned out tonight, Clay. What say we pick up from here tomorrow? You turning in yet?'

Rogan said he could be. Yet ten minutes later, after seeing the groggy peace officer off on his way home, he found himself standing across the street from the prosperous looking Cattlemen's Club where shaded lights still burned.

He checked his fob watch and frowned. One-fifteen. Clicking the piece shut, he moved on and turned along Baca Street which took him to the city square. As usual it was the last place in town where the dives were still doing business, the whores were toting their wares with diminishing optimism, and beggars still sat rattling their bowls and singing the praises of the Lord.

Leaning a shoulder against an upright he felt his pockets for the makings and gazed across at the mouth of the short laneway leading to the big old former hay barn which now went by its new name, the Centre.

Where dim lights showed behind the drawn curtains of the higher windows, they indicated, so he thought, that a governor's wife was likely still up there, occupied tending her charges.

Earlier the governor had taken him into his confidence and insisted he was working hard at repairing differences with his lady, but had not indicated if he were having any success. Rogan, despite an admittedly limited comprehension of how romances between regular men and women operated, had nodded and frowned seriously yet offered neither opinions or advice. Had he been forced to do so, he guessed he'd have felt obliged to suggest the governor still appeared to have a long way to go.

He did not pretend to know the ins and outs of that marriage, but knew from simple observation that Abel Fitzhenry was addicted to his work and seemed incapable of understanding why an attractive and intelligent woman might well feel that at least some of his attention might be profitably directed to herself.

He grinned, something he rarely did. Now, along with his new role as town-tamer Rogan, he was branching out as a romance adviser and expert!

He rolled and lit a smoke and was moving on when a door creaked open in the gloom somewhere close, bringing him to a halt.

'Who goes?' he called, right hand resting on gunbutt. The sound had come from a moon-shadowed yard which gave onto a side alley. A crumbling shed stood darkly in the yard, and he sensed furtive movement, then distinctly heard the scrape of a step.

In an instant he whipped out his .45 and hurled himself full length a split-second before the bellow of a six-shooter magnified by the late night hush of this murky backwater, breached the night's hush. Something small, swift and lethal whispered overhead before smashing violently into the doors of a decaying hay barn directly behind.

Fanning gun hammer, he drove five successive shots into the shed. He sprang erect as the gun echoes died, and detected the sound of swiftly receding steps.

Despite his size he could move fast when necessary. Even so, by the time he'd reached the rear of the shed, the laneway beyond was empty with gunsmoke hazing the gloom.

Reloading and breathing hard, he stood waiting and listening. Nothing. The beggars were still chanting, he could hear tin-panny music from a saloon across the square. And mused realistically: why should another barrage of shots more or less arouse Fitzhenry's turbulent city on the high plains?

Delaying only long enough to check out the clapboard shed, where he found nothing but an empty flask and a couple of cigarette butts, he returned to the plaza and found himself again looking towards the high, lighted windows of the Centre.

He didn't know what took him in that direction, and yet the impulse was strong. But before he got there, the doors of a somewhat better class of eatery swung open and he sighted the governor's aide emerge with a woman on his arm.

The moment he sighted his tall figure, Rade Tierney propped and scowled.

'Let me guess,' the man slurred. 'That shooting we just heard. That was the famous gunfighter from the south?'

'Keeping late hours, aren't you, Tierney?'

The man came forward, dragging the woman with him. He'd been drinking and his speech were slurred.

'You know, gunman, this place didn't need your kind to come horning in and trying to take over and big-noting himself—'

'Rade, don't make a fuss,' the woman urged.

'Who asked you?' Tierney snarled, and gave her a shove, causing her to trip and almost fall.

Next instant a big hand closed over his arm and he was slammed into an upright, almost causing him to go down.

Rogan poked him in the chest.

'That was assault, Tierney,' he grated. 'I could arrest you. Next time I will.'

The man swore, dragged the woman by the arm and lurched away. 'Borrowed time, gun shark! That's what you're living on, but it won't be for long!'

Rogan just shrugged and moved on. He saw the deputy governor as potentially dangerous, but how dangerous only time would tell.

He arrived at the Centre and climbed the stairs. No security. The governor's wife claimed her hospice for the poor and ill didn't need it. He supposed she was right. While public opinion on the governor might be mixed, Capital City seemed unanimous in the opinion his lady wife was some sort of angel.

The long, lamp-lit ward smelt of laudanum, disinfectant and humanity. Soon he found himself seated in the pokey little office sharing coffee with Isabel Fitzhenry with whom he seemed to have struck up an easy friendship.

He knew he enjoyed her company, but also suspected curiosity had a lot to do with his stopping by here from time to time. He'd known few people in his life who were genuinely unselfish and giving. This was a new experience for him.

He was leaving some time later when Carrie Morelos appeared suddenly from behind a screen She was toting a handbag, appeared exhausted, seemed puzzled to encounter him here and at such an hour.

He learned she had come in tonight to assist Isabel with a difficult patient. When he learned she was about to leave for home, Rogan insisted on escorting her, even felt obliged to start in lecturing as they descended the stairs.

'You shouldn't be running around on your own at this time of night, Carrie. Damnit, girl, I was shot at just minutes from here half an hour ago and—'

'Don't you start,' she cut in, bossy and assertive as usual. They reached the walkway. She nodded back at the building. 'Isabel nags me all the time.' She paused with an impish smile. 'I don't mind that, as we all know she's a saint. But I don't think that applies to you, do you?'

He was suddenly pleased they'd met. On the few occasions they'd been together he'd found her assertive, sure of herself, yet stimulating company. Most important, she appeared to find him simply odd, rather than somebody to cause her alarm or fear.

'Could you use a drink?' he heard himself ask.

'I thought you would never ask.' She gestured across the square. 'We'll go to the Silver Star. I'm very fond of the mint juleps they make there.'

Later, waiting for sleep to claim him, the gunfighter sat smoking and wondering if she had meant that one quick light kiss she gave when he escorted her to the house of her aunt on Maple Street.

And marvelled at the realization that he had not spared a thought for railroaders, cattlemen, the dry-gulcher who took pot-shots at him in back alleys, or even the past or the future for two full hours. A record!

Then he turned in to be asleep within minutes, that deep night towards the end of summer.

CHAPTER 7

GUN FOR HIRE

Mulligan knew he was in trouble the moment the saloon doors banged open and Big Sam Taylor came striding in. The Combine cattleman was rarely seen in squalid dumps like José's on this narrow side street, preferring the bigger, flashier saloons up there upon the square opposite the church where the women were prettier and the gambling stakes much higher.

The Cross Trail rancher did not glance Mulligan's way, at first. Instead, with two hard-faced cowhands trailing, the rancher crossed directly to the back bar where he slapped a meaty hand on the mahogany. He said loudly, 'Three shots for three thirsty men, bucko, and go easy on the sarsaparilla!'

That was meant to be a joke, for most real men like himself always took their whiskey straight. Someone laughed at his wit, the bartender poured – and Mulligan was suddenly wishing to hell he hadn't stopped by for a quick one before heading on home.

Home for Mulligan was a double section slab of land out along Caballero Creek in the shadow of treeless Vigil Hill.

The water was good at the creek, the grass only middling to fair. But Mulligan worked hard at rearing his small beef herd and it kept him and his family in vittles with a little play money left over, so he wasn't complaining.

Yet the truth was that his situation was tightening up by the week right now, just as fall was coming on. For mostly by this time of year he'd already sold his beef to the Combine and would now be cashed up at the Capital City bank as a result.

But this year, and for the very first time, he and a dozen or more small cattlemen just like himself were deliberately holding back from selling to the Combine, and he would bet hard money this was the reason Big Sam Taylor had chosen to slum it here today.

Taylor sat down heavily on a bar stool, sweating in an old-fashioned sourdough jacket. He jerked off his hat and swabbed his brow with a polka-dot kerchief.

He had a body slowly turning to suet, yet still powerful. A man who used to ride a lot but didn't do so as much these days. Success was likely the reason for that, Mulligan mused. For Sam Taylor's position as a full partner in the powerful three-man Cattle Combine which had dominated the beef industry here for well over a decade, was an iron-clad guarantee of prosperity.

Years earlier, the three major ranches of the

region had joined together to form the Combine, and immediately assumed control of the beef industry. Twice every year now the Combine bought up the smaller spreads' stock at low prices, added their own few cows to the mobs then drove the combined herd across twenty miles of rough and risky country to the railhead up at Larribee.

In the early days some small ranchers had attempted to rebel against the system and sever their dependence on the Combine by setting out to herd their own stock to the railhead, in order that they might get paid what they were worth, not whatever pittance the Combine might toss their way.

Invariably these attempts ended in disaster and often bloodshed. None ever got through. The Combine was believed to be behind the raids but this was never proven or disproven. After several such bloody failures the small cattlemen finally had no option but to go back to the Combine, who punished them for their 'rebelliousness' by paying even less than before.

From then on the Combine had seemed as solid as anything a man could build, until relatively recently when the 'R' word had intruded on Capital County. R, as in Railroad.

For several years prior to this eventful summer the cowed small cattlemen had been selling all their stock to the Combine which then drove the resulting huge herds up to the railhead at Larribee at huge profit.

Until this year. This was the year and the summer when the railroad would finally come to Capital City

and men like Mulligan would be free to run their
stock down to the handsome newly erected yards
right here and have dealers and buyers from all over
bidding for their beef.

Naturally the Combine reacted when they realized
what was taking place, and that some of the smaller
men were holding out on them. There had been
threats, the occasional rancher shot at from ambush,
and any number of warning ultimatums issued from
the plush Cattlemen's Club upon the square.

But Mulligan, like his fellow ranchers, had made a
point of keeping well clear of the Combiners wherever possible as the track-end inched closer and
tensions mounted.

Now suddenly he was here alone in a saloon,
where Taylor unexpectedly heaved himself off his
stool with a windy grunt and was toting his shot glass
across the room towards him!

Why in hell had he stopped for this shot?

'So . . . drinking it up in the middle of the day, just
like a rich feller, eh, Mulligan?' The big man stood
before his table with a hard-faced hand on either
flank. 'You know, I always thought only rich folk
could afford that. That must mean you're rich, or
maybe just expecting to get that way. Would that be
how it is, Mulligan, old pard?'

Panic gripped the rancher. He made a sudden
reckless dive for the batwings, but a tripping foot
caught his leg and he went down. As he made to rise
a heavy number ten boot slammed into his back,
sending pain shooting through to his bootheels.

The voice seemed to come from a great distance.

'We're expecting you and your beef at the Double X by midday tomorrow, Mulligan. If it ain't, you and your brood will be sleeping under a tree tomorrow night – if you are still breathing, that is.' His gesture swept the silent room. 'This goes for the rest of you smartass, double-dealing sons of bitches. Forget the railroad and forget the law. We can squash you like bugs if we've a mind. But for old time's sake we'll still take your lousy cows off your hands and run them to Larribee just like always. And if you're lucky you'll still get your cut even though you planned to cross us.'

Another kick.

'Midday, tomorrow!' Mulligan heard before he passed out.

The horse was beginning to play out a little before midday. Kip Silver was making good time but knew he must spell up shortly. The table land on which Capital City stood was several thousand feet higher than the baking plains he'd left far behind him, and his fat mare was making heavy weather of the climb.

So he shrugged and jerked on the reins to change directions. He rode down through the piñon and aspen dotted foothills until sighting the village.

It was a small and unremarkable scatter of dwellings flanked by the dribbling creek which eventually emptied into Roaring River, sixty miles to the north-west.

Small mud huts dotted either side of the stream and a buck naked kid of about three shrieked and

109

ran like hell when he glanced up and saw him come splashing across.

He grinned. He liked to scare people. Only thing, sometimes he frightened folks – like pretty women for instance – when he didn't wish to.

He believed it was his name and reputation that had this effect, even though this bare-assed brat wouldn't know him from Wild Bill Hickok. But he knew he was both handsome and famous, so what else could it be but fear that seemed to make some folks want to avoid him?

The woman, the young girl and the kid all stared out at him wide-eyed from the dark mouth of their mud hut as he reined in and slid to ground, bouncing a little as his boots touched earth.

Then the old man appeared from the horse yard, and forced a snaggle-toothed grin of welcome.

'Señor Silver! Welcome to my humble home, welcome!'

'Water and grub,' grunted Silver, eyes devouring the girl. She looked good. But that was as far as it would go, he thought with a sigh. It was still a far ways to Capital City, and with the mare slower than usual he would have no choice but to keep riding, even if he would rather get to rest up and maybe get to chase that young one through the chaparral.

Another time, he promised himself.

His eyes turned cold again as he signalled for coffee before seeking the shade of a miserable tree. At his last stopover he'd heard enough biggety talk about Rogan to turn his stomach. Although it seemed hard to believe, it sounded like Rogan had really landed on his feet up there. Silver had learned the governor had granted him amnesty then signed him on for a job walking the streets and scaring away the wild men . . . or so the jawbones had it.

It was galling. And yet, he realized perversely as he stood sipping his coffee and ogling the girl, it was also exactly how he hoped to find things when he got there. For Rogan walking tall was just how he wanted that big son of a bitch. He would just have that much further to fall when his time came.

Suddenly he felt fully restored and eager to get underway again. He didn't bother thanking anybody, just gave the girl a wink then rode away, thinking; 'I might have taken you with me if you'd played up to me some, sweetheart . . . still, that's your big loss. . . .'

He splashed across the tired brown stream and pointed the fat mare north. It was still a long way to Capital City. He might have kicked the mare into a trot, but didn't. He realized he was now savouring the expectation of riding into that sprawling table land city and waiting for their reaction. He hadn't been there in quite a spell . . . that last time when he hunted Fast Jimmy Cade down there and shot him dead on the square.

That was a good memory to occupy himself with as the long horse miles fell behind.

Rogan hit the saloon floor hard, but was still a long way from being hurt. Spinning as he struck the boards, he sensed rather than saw the kick from the big black boot that grazed his brow before crashing into the floorboards. In an instant he was back on his feet, shaking his head to clear it and bobbing defensively as a hairy fist whistled by his jaw.

He swayed back a step, hatless, bleeding from one corner of his mouth, but well-balanced and beginning to see clearly once again.

The heavyweight farm labourer came charging in, intent on finishing Rogan off before he could fully recover from the sneak punch crashed to the back of his neck as he entered the Santo Domingo Cantina on Perod Street.

Rogan made it seem easy the way he swayed out of reach of that wild swing, then allowed his attacker's momentum to carry him onto the short right hook to the jaw which he threw with perfect timing and maximum impact.

The attacker's boots actually left the floor and he crashed flat onto his back with an impact that shook the dust down from the spider-haunted rafters.

To the man's credit, he spat blood and teeth and struggled his way up onto one knee, still cursing, still intent on finishing what he'd started.

It was a case of ambition outstripping ability. As the big ugly head rose to the level of Rogan's belt buckle, the brawler was caught by a second and heavier punch that smashed him flat, out to the world.

Silence.

Mere moments earlier the Santo Domingo on noisome Perod Street had been abuzz with rough laughter, the chink of glassware punctuated by a woman's drunken shriek – all the sounds of life to be expected in any Capital City liquor joint after sundown. Now shopworn women and nervous men began edging away from the batwings to make plenty space for the governor's new man to stoop and collect his hat.

Rogan dusted the flat brim off then let his tongue explore his mouth. One tooth loose, but not dislodged. Could be worse.

And thought: 'Be warned, amnesty man. You were careless for a moment there . . . and it could just as easily have been a bullet as a smack in the jaw. . . .'

He nodded soberly then put a hard stare upon the drinkers.

'All right, let's hear it,' he said. He jabbed a finger at a runt with ears like a bat. 'You! Who is he?'

The man had to swallow twice before finding his voice. 'Er . . .'Chisum off of Double X Ranch . . . Mister Marshal sir. Just afore you showed he said he was sick of hearing how big and tough you were and all—'

'I can fill in the rest. You four! Yeah . . . you! Cart him across the square to the law office and tell the sheriff to lock him up. I'll file charges later.' His eyes cut to a single steely gleam as he swept his gaze around the hushed room. 'Somebody could have warned me. I'll remember that next time any of you get into trouble, as you surely will.'

Eyes evaded his own, heads hung sheepishly. 'That goes double for you,' he rapped to the saloonkeeper, then turned and shouldered his way out into the night.

He'd appeared genuinely angry, yet this wasn't the case. Emotion was a luxury which neither a gunfighter or even an interim peace officer could rightly afford. Experience had taught him so. As a consequence he was totally calm and alert as he started across the plaza square in the early evening.

The sheriff would see to it that his attacker drew a month behind bars. He would leave Tom Doherty to raise the matter with his attacker's boss, Logan Osgood, next time the Double X rancher showed in town. The matter was not important enough to be taken any further. This week and the next would be dominated exclusively by those twin steel tracks inching closer and closer from the west every day now, and he had a part to play in deciding whether or not that enterprise succeeded or failed.

The stakes were high and growing higher.

The Combine had controlled the entire cattle industry here for many years during which it was guilty of everything from rustling to brand-blotting to intimidating honest small ranchers into selling them their beef for next to nothing while they had prospered. Seemed at times they had not even balked at murder.

But from that historical moment when the first loco came snorting into the depot and marshalling yards, now under construction and nearing completion directly to the west of the city square, all buying and selling would be carried out by legitimate agents under the watchful eye of the law. And come the first big cattle auction, the governor, his soldiers and lawmen, along with his new enforcer, would combine to ensure that the Double X, Cross Trail and Epic ranches would find it difficult to sell a single head of beef until every little man whom they'd harried and cheated for so long had his moment and his cattle under the auctioneer's hammer first.

The crowded square was unaware of what had just transpired at the saloon.

With dust raised by wheels and feet hazing the many lights, with music blaring and the night air filled with the cries of tradesmen, hucksters and children who should be home in bed all blending in with the groan of wheels and clatter of hoofs. This was the place to buy, sell, fight, fall in love or just go to hell in your own easy way, and nobody would give much of a damn which route you chose.

He filled his head with the smells and was barely conscious of his headache now. He was invigorated by the myriad odours of this Spanish-American city of the high plains filling the air – the scents of humanity, tortillas, wine, beans, horses, sweating Indians, piñon and cooking meat. He heard the laughter, the cursing, singing, quacking and braying punctuated by the occasional scream or shriek. There was the clatter of roulette wheels and the thrum of deep-throated guitars in the soft night.

And wondered if he stayed here long enough might he over time eventually wind down sufficiently until he became just as lazy, indolent – and as happy – as any of them?

He moved on slowly and occasionally someone might either pat his shoulder approvingly or yell something ugly behind his back.

He welcomed both alike, for this proved the city's vitality, which he was fast coming to believe could be channelled into peace and prosperity one day – providing they got their railroad, the Combine was curbed, and the government remained steadfast and strong.

This last thought gave rise to another, and he decided to make his way back at the mansion and see how Fitzhenry was faring. He hoped the governor and his lady might get to patch up their differences before the big day. But when he stopped by the mansion it was to find the governor alone and slumped morosely in a deep cane chair on his front gallery with bottle and glass.

Rogan still had plenty of tasks to attend to. But after massaging the back of his head and accepting a glass of the good wine, he decided he'd likely done enough for one day.

He sat until late listening to Fitzhenry speak eloquently about love, failure, success, railroads and retirement. Mostly Rogan simply nodded or grunted occasionally and was surprised how often his thoughts strayed, not to cattle or railroads nor even the old days with the guns. Instead he found himself thinking of a woman with dazzling dark eyes who honestly seemed to believe a man like him could easily change his spots, and what she called, 'settle down to a normal life'. If he really wished.

Carrie Morelos was an enigma, he mused, while the governor droned on. She had more spirit than most anyone he knew and spoke straight from the shoulder. He admired the way she used her relative affluence to help out folks, such as the patients at the Centre. And thought . . . if things were different, if I was something else, like a lawyer or merchant or such, then maybe. . . .

He pulled himself up right there. He looked down and saw only a man with a gun, even if he might well be far different from that man who'd first quit Fort Such to make his way north.

Eventually he interrupted the governor's monologue and proposed a toast to the railroad and the future of the territory. And both men drank deep.

CHAPTER 8

CAME THE
NIGHT RIDER

It was late when Carrie Morelos had the handyman bring her stylish rig round to the side door of the Centre. He yawned hugely while handing her up, excused himself then hung onto the reins a moment as she settled into her seat.

'Sure you don't want me to escort you home, miss? This town ain't no different tonight than any other. Still full of drunks and trouble and—'

'Clarry, when I start getting scared, I'll stay home and become the proper young lady my father is always urging me to be.'

He let go the lines and stepped back a pace with a tired smile. 'Guess you know best, little lady.'

She was about to wheel away when she check-reined with a frown. 'I just remembered. Did some-

118

one say you heard something about Marshal Rogan tonight, Clarry?'

He grinned.

'Sure did, missy. Feller jumped him in a saloon, and got his head busted for his trouble. Hey, hey.'

'Is the Marshal all right?'

'Saw him strolling by an hour back. He looked chipper enough to me.'

'Yet he didn't stop by—?'

'Pardon, missy?'

'Never mind,' she said, slapping the reins and wheeling away. 'You get straight to bed now.'

She smiled when she glanced back to see the stooped figure trudging obediently back for his quarters. But she was serious again when she swung into the square minutes later where the high-livers, hard drinkers, the gamblers, girls of the night and all the shuffling bums were still abroad in numbers. And wondered if things would change all that much after the railroad came.

She doubted it.

For Capital City had its own unique character and she wasn't even sure she wanted that part of it ever to change, for as it was, it was exciting, unpredictable, and continued to attract all sorts of interesting people.

And, of course, she was forced to remind herself – it was also a magnet for the hopelessly violent, drunken and desperate. Then there were all those many who were eternally fearful. Of the railroad, the Cattle Combine and the criminals and killers who walked its streets. Some were even afraid of those purporting to represent law and order.

Law and order?

She frowned. Was she thinking about him again? This annoyed her as it often did. Yet it had been this way for her ever since his arrival two weeks earlier, all tall and sombre with that big gun riding his hip. He crept into her thoughts at the oddest times whether at home, out having a good time or occasionally helping out at the Centre.

It really was most aggravating, she thought, compressing her lips. Then she swore – just another habit her father disapproved of – when she found herself for some reason taking the first side street off the plaza to go driving past the jailhouse.

The lights were on in the long low building and she saw the glow of cigarettes in the gloom of the porch. She slowed deliberately, at the same time berating herself for whatever it might be she thought she was doing.

She failed to listen to herself. Instead, upon drawing level with the jailhouse, she slowed the horse to a walk and pretended to be glancing backwards to check out her rear wheel.

She was almost past the building when she heard the voice, 'Need any help there, lady?'

She reined in and glanced back over her shoulder to see the familiar tall figure emerging from the darkened porch. And thought, 'Surely I must be crazy!' Yet immediately, she heard herself say, 'I thought I struck a stone— Oh, it's you.'

He stood beside the rig and removed his hat. 'Carrie? Do you know what time it is?'

'Don't start. I'm sick of people telling me what to—' She broke off sharply, staring. 'What's that mark on your forehead, Mr Rogan?'

'You've been calling me Clay—'

'The bruise. Oh, yes, I do believe I can guess. More trouble for the new city marshal? I thought you said it was more a pretend job in order that Governor Fitzhenry could show you off as an example of how well his amnesty can work, yet with no real danger involved? Yet the next thing I hear you are brawling in saloons – really! And what are you grinning at?'

He was smiling because he was pleased. Maybe it was just coincidence that had brought her through here at this time of night, but he wanted to believe otherwise. 'We can discuss that on the way home . . . if you'll just move over?'

'I'm perfectly capable of—' she began, then found herself with no option but to slide across the seat as he climbed up and took the reins. 'Really!'

'Corner of North and Lopez Street . . . right?' he said, slapping the reins.

He didn't catch her response. Neither did Sheriff Tom Doherty, standing in the gloom of his unlit porch. The lawman scratched his head as the buggy vanished round the corner. He yawned hugely, was about to head off for home and bed, when from the square came the bellow of a gunshot followed by drunken laughter.

He sighed as he went in, collected hat and riot gun and trudged off to investigate. Everyone had a dream of how things might change when the railroad came. He confined himself to the single frail hope that when law and order were fully restored maybe folks here might start keeping regular hours so a man could get some sleep.

Squinting through his binoculars from the second floor window of the Cattlemen's Club, Combiner Mike Quinn found he could now actually see it. Until recently that gap in the hills west of the city was all rough country without any dwellings or improvements due to its rocky nature, yet today it was swarming with activity.

He estimated he could make out upwards of a score of coolie workers swinging picks and bars amongst the rocks up there. And, higher up, other small, dark-haired figures were to be seen hacking into the scatter of ugly trees dotting both sides of the gap.

Yet all this was as nothing compared to that glinting metal silhouette he could dimly see as it stood in the sunlight probing the dust clouds beyond the work gang.

His breath caught in his throat as he beckoned dramatically. 'Look at this – I swear to Judas I never believed I'd live to see this black day!'

Big Sam Taylor reached him first and snatched the glasses. Fitting them to his eyes, he adjusted the setting then seemed to sag as though something within had collapsed. Wordlessly he passed the instrument to Osgood, who went motionless when able to make out, first that fat black smokestack, then the gleaming metal flanks of the work loco where it stood motionless upon the tracks, snorting dirty smoke into the sky.

Of course they'd known it was coming for a long time, had fought it, sought to undermine it, had even lost men in their failed attempts to dynamite those ever-extending twin ribbons of steel.

All to no effect.

Yet even though they had been acutely aware of the new technology reaching closer and closer, today's sighting came as a shock to the senses, all that timber, stone, steel and billowing smoke and dust a dramatic reminder of how dismally they had failed to protect their enforced monopoly of the cattle trade here for so long.

And that was the moment, as the inarguable reality finally struck home, that they found themselves forced to sit down facing one another in their fat leather cushioned chairs and almost concede defeat – while at the same time sheeting home the blame.

'Fitzhenry,' Quinn rumbled, paler than they'd ever seen him. 'We took him to be just a flash-in-the-pan ladder-climber looking to serve his time here and get out just as quick as he got a better government appointment—'

'I reckon it's been more that stinking Fort Such gunslinger they brought in right when we were making headway against the track layers,' Big Sam Taylor interrupted. 'Judas Priest! He pins on a badge, pistol whips a few drunks and next thing them hick ranchers are holding off trading their beef to us so they can hold out for the line to be finished when they can sell on the open market. And we've even got men too scared to come to town for fear of getting beat up or arrested. You look back. That's when it started slipping away on us. With the wrong bastard getting handed their lousy amnesty!'

'Well, ain't you got nothing to say?' Quinn snapped at Logan Osgood.

'Only that we ain't just going to sit here and watch that freaking train come clanking in here and take away our livelihood,' came the bitter response. 'Hear me? We just ain't!'

They heard loud and clear. Yet they did not believe. And deep inside, Osgood, the Combine leader who had once dominated the law, the small ranchers and even this city itself, knew that he could not believe his own words They had held power, abused it, then were suddenly confronted by a power they could not handle and then found that they lacked the courage, the will or even the knowhow to try to claw their way back.

For the former kings of the cattle country, just talking now seemed all they could do.

The horseman made his way across the sagging West Bridge to enter the city in the darkest depth of the night, the fat mare stumbling a little from exhaustion yet responding to his touch to her neck.

For now the animal could finally smell something other than sagebrush and dust, and there were murmuring sounds somewhere ahead that spoke of shelter, hay, clean water and escape from the sun.

Kip Silver knew the horse was exhausted. He could sympathize yet not share in the animal's misery. For despite the brutal journey from the south the killer was brimming with energy and exhilarated by images of triumph upon finding himself at long last to be riding into Capital City.

His final stopover before making the last push up-trail had been at a small farm town where he'd been able to shave, wash and make a few essential purchases. Another traveller might have been content with that without fitting himself out with an entirely new wardrobe before showing up at the capital. But style and polish were as important as food and drink to the man from Fort Such on what might prove to be his crowning achievement.

Kill Rogan.

His clean-shaven jaw set hard as he tugged lightly back on the reins then slid to ground on the city side of the river. Rogan had destroyed everything, he mused bitterly. The camaraderie of the gunfighters, the old life at Fort Such. Merely by saddling up and riding out, the big man had exposed the emptiness of the killers' lives, and one by one they had drifted and disappeared, leaving the saloon to just a sad-eyed bartender – and Kip Silver.

There was noplace else for Silver to go. He had no old home town, no faithful woman waiting for him, had never boasted a genuine friend. Nor was there any peaceful retreat where he might get to hang up his shooters as others had done, grow fat and sit around boasting about the great old days.

Fort Such was all he'd had. This despite the hard truth that he'd never been liked there and had made no friends. Nor had he even received the kudos as top gun, a title he'd always known he'd deserved.

Instead, to a man, they had treated Rogan like he was top dog. And even when that big bastard turned Judas Iscariot and headed north to suck up to the governor for a pardon and a pat on the head, they refused to condemn him, but meekly decided the game was all over and shut up shop.

And in doing so, shut down on his life.

He shuddered, cursed bitterly just the once, then immediately became strong again.

For all could yet be redeemed. He'd always been the gun king and now destiny was calling upon him to prove it, once and forever. And now he was seeing things in that clear light he felt eager and ready to bring about a resolution of the grievances that had brought him here – to this grand stage.

For Fort Such had always been little more than just a wide place in the trail, distinguished only by a bunch of bloody-handed gunmen, a notorious reputation, and little else.

Capital City, by contrast, was the territory's rapidly expanding centre of trade, commerce, politics and power. The perfect stage upon which to strut his finest hour in the harsh glare of the publicity spotlight that would see his name emblazoned across the West!

The mare swung its head and nudged his knee. The gunman blinked as though coming out of a trance. He swung down and laughed softly at himself, something he rarely did. 'Settle down, gunfighter!' he murmured. Then proceeded to pace around the patient animal until he was feeling cool, relaxed and in full control again. Still smiling beneath his

126

hatbrim at the sure knowledge of what it was like to be the best of the best.

Rogan, he realized, as he swung lightly back into the saddle and moved the horse on with a light pressure of his heels, would be number seventeen.

CHAPTER 9

FORT SUCH REMEMBERED

Rogan hit the saddle before daylight and was riding well clear of Capital City by the time the sun winked into life in the east.

There was a slight chill in the air today, a reminder that the days were shortening. He reined in atop Bald Hill to watch the city slowly stir into life, then slapped the reins and pushed on for the cattle country to the south-west.

The horse was sweating by the time he reached the boundary of the Double X Ranch an hour later. He reined in on a wooded knoll and sat his saddle, allowing his gaze to play over some of the finest rangeland in the region. Out here, a half mile from the ranch headquarters situated further along the creek, there were less than a dozen fat cattle grazing upon a pasture which could well feed a hundred. In the distance he spotted a nighthawk, riding back for breakfast.

A classic, peaceful rural scene. So, what else had he expected?

He wasn't sure. Yet he had first ridden out here in the early morning of the previous day, and would likely do the same thing again tomorrow. The Combine ranchers had been raising all kinds of hell in town, even petitioning the governor against the railroad and firing off telegrams to important people they believed could still stop the railroad construction even at the eleventh hour.

All of which was legitimate, he supposed. Yet the Combine's murky history, which was fully recorded both at the governor's mansion and the jailhouse, surely bordered on the criminal. Having laboriously worked his way through the bulk of this relevant documentation on the three spreads during the past week, Rogan had come away with the conviction that all the ugly accusations levelled against the Combine by the small ranchers who'd suffered most at their hands, were most likely true.

Extortion, market manipulation, even the unsolved murders of several small cattlemen who'd battled against the Combine in the past. It was all there in the records and in many cases appeared to point the finger of suspicion strongly in the Combine's direction. Yet few charges had ever been laid against the big men. Puzzled by this, Rogan had investigated several failed court actions brought by the ranchers against the Combine. He had come away believing that in virtually all of the aborted cases it seemed only too plain that it was coercion, bribery or even the blatant corruption of the judiciary which had saved the big three from conviction and punishment, time after time.

Sheriff Doherty, straight and honest yet nowhere near capable of dealing with an organization as ruthless and powerful as the Combine, had told Rogan to his face that he considered Osgood, Taylor and Quinn the three biggest crooks in Southwest County. And then had added gloomily, 'But like they say, what good does it do a man to know that it's wolves that are killing his cattle if he doesn't have any blamed idea how to snare them?'

Meaning, that the Combine was too tough to handle. Or leastways this had been the case before Governor Fitzhenry found the courage to authorize the building of the controversial spur line from Larribee.

Sitting his saddle and rolling a smoke, Rogan was almost certain that Fitzhenry had never expected the building of the line actually to survive all the attacks and incidents of sabotage that had thus far marked its construction. The grit and tenacity of the Line and its workers had astonished everyone, and just this week the railroad had finally powered its way to within sight of the city, to the elation of a hundred quarter-section cattlemen and the astonishment and delight of an entire city.

So, if things were looking so positive, then why was amnesty Marshal Clay Rogan sitting his horse ten miles from town wearing a heavy frown, when he could be just lowering himself into a chair at Midge

Riddle's to attack one of her famous three-course breakfasts?

The answer to that was, he wasn't sleeping like he should. He could not sleep because 'it' kept him awake and restless. His sixth sense, that was. It had been nagging him worse every day lately. It was three days now since unknown gunmen had last attacked the railroad workings, and far from being reassured by this seeming lull in the violence Rogan was growing increasingly edgy and suspicious.

He lighted up another and reviewed the full picture of past events in his mind to see if he was overlooking something.

As he understood it all, the Combine had first seized control of the entire beef industry by brute force and intimidation, then channelled that industry into a mould of their making. It was a twenty-mile drive through dangerous Indian country up to the railhead at Larribee, far too risky for a single rancher or even a dozen to try to attempt, and so they had eventually quit. As a consequence, the small ranchers were half starving when the Combine threw them a 'lifeline'. Twice a year from then on, the Combine mustered a bunch of tough gunmen-drovers, bought up all the small rancher's stock for a song, then trail-drove up to the cattle yards in Larribee on the rail-road where they were able to sell at a huge profit.

He'd learned that the big three grew so wealthy with this scheme they barely bothered raising any of their own stock any more – and he was looking at proof of that here today in the almost empty graze lands. And why should they bother? They could buy up all the marketable cattle they could drive without raising so much as a single steer of their own if they didn't want to. They had the beef industry all sewn up, leaving them free to dabble in finance, politics and luxury living.

But then came the unexpected when a surveyor employed by the Great Southwest Railroad showed up in Capital City to announce the railroad would shoot a trunk line though a rough chunk of territory from Larribee to the capital and so make it the shipping centre of the entire region, spelling the end of the Combine's strangle hold on the market.

The Great Southwest had proven as good as its word and blood had been spilled along the tracks of the high iron as the desperate Combine first succeeded but then ultimately failed to halt construction.

Today the tracks were drawing inexorably closer. Drawing nearer also was that final day when, with construction completed, the outside beef buyers would proceed to tap into the non-Combine market by paying fair prices to the small ranchers for first-grade beef.

But what could the Combine do now? This was what he must figure. He couldn't believe they'd take such a crushing defeat lying down.

He'd ridden out today hoping to see or hear something that could offer a clue to their plans; he thought the silence and clean air might stimulate his thinkbox.

This had not happened.

There was nothing to see out here. Either the

Combine genuinely intended simply to accept defeat and allow the railroad and small cattlemen to walk all over them. Either that, or they were playing their cards closer to their chest than he had the savvy to figure out.

His mood was heavy as he set off on a long loop through the back country which would eventually take him to the railroad's construction office situated some ten miles west of the city.

He was impressed by what he encountered there. The efficient and straightforward chief engineer in command welcomed him as a pro-railroader and a valuable ally. As did later another official with wide experience in dealing with the challenges and problems invariably associated with the huge technology of any railroad storming into some backwater and bringing along with it all the advantages and problems of the modern era.

It was mid-afternoon before he set off along the incomplete stretch of glittering new tracks that would take him home. He felt almost a twinge of personal pride when Capital City finally came into view. He'd helped out plenty here, he knew. Too bad he didn't have the developed skills a genuine lawman would surely possess that might enable him to get rid of that itch in his brain he couldn't get to scratch.

Even now, sitting his mount with the sights and scents and colour of the city drifting up to him, he felt vaguely edgy. Yet why should he feel anything but buoyant on a day when everything seemed to be going like clockwork?

He spent time with the track-end workers and officials then drifted on into the city which, up close, looked, sounded, smelt and felt exactly as it had done every day since his arrival.

Yet he detected something in the air that caused that old familiar tingling in his wrists which he always associated with danger of some kind.

And his instincts, so constantly honed over so many dangerous years, rarely let him down.

This warned him that trying to shrug off this premonition was a waste of time, and maybe could prove fatal.

Something *was* not right, and it was the duty of any city marshal to find out what.

His first thought was for the Centre. He headed off there immediately but found everything as it should be, with several charity workers helping out there while Mrs Fitzhenry and Carrie took a late lunch someplace.

He went back outside where life stirred languidly in the hot mid-afternoon. He massaged the back of his neck. It was still there, that sensation. Maybe he should go check at the jailhouse? He did so, finding the sheriff dozing in his chair and enjoying one of the quietest days he'd had in weeks.

Cussing and peevish by this, Rogan rode off to the mansion where he found everything proceeding so efficiently that all the governor wanted to discuss with him was his marriage, along with the problem of whether or not he should remain in Capital City after the railroad was safely bedded down, or if he should seek further promotion. What did Rogan think?

Rogan quit the office without a word and set out

on a one-man patrol of all the major trouble spots in town, an operation that used up a sweaty two hours and did not even offer him the chance to break up a single drunken brawl.

Peace reigned in volatile Capital City. If there was a single jarring note it was one tetchy marshal who folks thought was acting like he'd eaten something that didn't agree with him.

That was when he began thinking about food and realized he'd not broken his fast since daylight and it was now mid-afternoon!

Satisfied he'd finally identified the simple reason for his edginess, he forced a grin and strode off along the winding side street that brought him quickly to the square close by the Hotel Grande and the Cross Hatch Café.

He was headed directly for the eatery but didn't get that far. As he emerged from beneath the high verandah of the hotel he sighted a bunch of people standing before him, all peering upwards and pointing.

Curious, he propped and glanced up.

A man stood above him leaning against an upright with arms folded and a cigarette angling from smiling white teeth as he acknowledged the attentions of the rapidly swelling crowd.

It was Kip Silver.

'You're jittery, big man. You never used to be that way, as I recall. Must be all these strange and unnatural ways they say you've taken to up here. You know? Beating up on drunks and sitting up at the mansion nights swigging French wine with your new pal, the governor. Surely that's no way for a red-blooded six-gun wonder to be carrying on. Do you figure all this pretending to be something you ain't, might be starting to tell on you some?'

Rogan completed fashioning his cigarette into a neat cylinder in silence. His hands were rock steady. Around him, the gloomy bar room of the Bonanza Saloon was unnaturally quiet. By this the identity of the two-gun newcomer to Capital City had been relayed across the plaza and beyond. A few had seen Kip Silver here in the past, mostly when he was passing through on his way from one place to another on some mysterious business of his own. Some claimed the 'Kipper' had killed a man here once, but nobody seemed able to recollect the details.

Only when his cigarette was drawing to his satisfaction did Rogan rest one elbow on the bar and look the other in the eye.

Silver seemed different.

He'd thought this at first glance out on the square; it was even more noticeable up close. This difference was hard to define at first. As usual, the killer appeared relaxed and supremely sure of himself. He acted amiable enough but Rogan was not buying that. There had to be a reason for the man who hated him to show up here just as Capital City was steamrolling towards a defining moment in its history.

Trouble and Kip Silver had been trail partners as far back as anyone could recall. The six-gunner had already made it plain he regarded Rogan's seeking amnesty as a gross act of disloyalty to the brother-hood back in the desert. Rogan had heard that his quitting Fort Such had been interpreted by his gun brothers as a sign the old days were over. It seemed as if in the wake of his departure some sort of quit-ting disease infected the habitués of Charron's Bar, and that one by one and day by day, the gun gods of Lonesome River strapped their bedrolls on their horses, made their goodbyes and faded away into the dust and heat.

Until only Charron was left to drink his own lousy whiskey and stand alone at his long bar listening in vain for the sound of one of his wild ones returning, and might still be waiting there even now.

Studying the sleek killer, Rogan saw new lines in his face and the different look in his eye. It was a jolt to realize the killer looked like a man who was griev-ing!

This cold killer?

He shook his head. Must be something simpler, he decided. Simple hate was far more likely to have brought him here and put that steely glint in his eye.

And mused wonderingly, had Fort Such been all this killer ever had?

One thing was certain. Silver hadn't arrived here by chance. So, why?

It was a good question. 'Let me guess, mister. You've taken a contract to blast someone here?' he said evenly.

'If that was so I'd be doing it for a fee a hundred times more than what you get for sporting that farty little tin badge in your lapel. Big man!'

137

You had to hand it to Kip Silver. Outwardly he appeared as relaxed and self-assured as if he were propping up a bar in Fort Such. Only someone who knew him could tell he was riding a lightning bolt of anger and emotion, a killer on a short rein.

'All right,' Rogan said, suddenly impatient now. 'So I heard that Fort Such fell apart and that you blamed me for that. I also learned you nearly got yourself killed recent and so might be down on your luck. So why don't you tell me the truth about what made you ride a hundred miles across the desert just to look me in the eye? And don't hand me any bull-dust, savvy?'

'Well, glory be, Aunt Martha! I didn't expect you to get all cross and bothered—'

'I said talk straight!' Rogan's voice filled the room. The more time slipped by the sharper the stink of danger. And with that came the realization that this was one of the very few times in his six-gunner's life when he'd sensed he could be in a situation that might cost his life.

For this man was that good. Or that bad, depending on your point of view.

He straightened to full height and willed his heartbeat to slow down. His fingertips began to tingle. At that very moment, he was as ready to kill as he'd ever been. 'Enough bulldust, Silver! If you've got some grief with me either spit it out or back it up!'

Seconds stalked the eye-locked silence. The quiet spread to engulf the entire room as two motionless men faced across ten feet of cigarette littered floor. A man coughed with dreadful dryness and a hooker's pet cat scooted for a side door.

Rogan felt himself blink when the killer abruptly laughed.

'Ahh, big man. Still playing up to the gallery, I see.'

His gaze swept the bar room and not a man appeared to breathe.

'Sorry to disappoint all you gutless scum!' he said with slow venom. 'But the time just ain't right. But when it is, you're sure gonna know it!'

Suppressed rage was leaking from the corners of the killler's eyes as he directed one last stare at an impassive Rogan before striding out into the night, batwings flapping to silence in back of him.

Rogan slowly relaxed his big body. He hefted his glass and drained the last of the good whiskey. At least now he was certain of one thing. Silver *had* come here to kill him.

'Don't miss with your first shot, Kip,' he murmured. And in that moment Clay Rogan looked far more gunslinger than peacekeeper.

'Oh, I'm sorry, Isabel,' Carrie said. 'I've spilled the water—'

'It's all right dear, I was just about to give Señor Rico a purge – which is about the last thing the poor man requires.'

Carrie Morelos's dark eyes crinkled at the corners. She suppressed a giggle, then flushed with embarrassment. There was kindness and care aplenty to combat all the illness and suffering at the Centre, but rarely laughter, particularly not in front of the patients in the ward, as they were now.

The governor's wife made to reprove the younger woman. Then understanding struck. She suspected that Carrie, although almost laughing, was actually on the verge of tears.

'Nurse Judy!' she called. 'Carrie and I are through for the night. Will you kindly take over?'

The olive-skinned assistant nodded and smiled. The two women in their white coveralls quit the ward and went through to the balcony to look towards the plaza.

'I'm sorry, Isabel. I don't know what came over me.'

'I know. A woman can't nurse and worry herself sick at the same time. Would you care for a drink of something strong, honey?'

'How strong?'

By way of response the governor's wife disappeared into the rest room and reappeared shortly afterwards clutching two glasses filled with hospital brandy.

'Drink this and forget about him for the moment,' Isabel said sternly.

'I beg your pardon—'

'Your mind has been someplace else ever since we heard of what happened at the saloon.' Isabel sighed. 'And I can't say I blame you. I felt – feel, that should Clay and this awful man fight, as everybody seems to believe they will, it might destroy everything here. I know Abel has been worried something violent could erupt ever since that gunman rode in. He says the whole city has been waiting for something to trigger it off due to all the tension and hostility over the railroad, and that this could prove what he calls the catalyst which might even destroy the city itself.'

'Ruby says he's killed more than twenty men. Surely that is an exaggeration?'

'Perhaps not, dear.' The governor's wife shook her head. 'I just couldn't believe what I heard at the mansion today. When Rade Tierney heard about the incident at the saloon, he suggested to Abel that he might head off serious trouble by dismissing Clay Rogan, claiming he is actually the trouble here and not this gunman.'

'What did the governor say?'

Isabel suddenly smiled. 'He sacked him, right then and there. Oh, I was so proud of him. I never liked Rade Tierney and – oh, what's happening over yonder by the church?'

Carrie followed her gesture to sight a surging mass of brawling figures suddenly erupt from a vacant lot to go punching and kicking their way down a laneway leading onto the square. Suddenly a shot rang out and somebody screamed.

'That's it! the girl gasped. 'All this talk of a gunfight and what the cattlemen might do to the railroad has whipped the town into violence! Oh, Isabel, the city can't absorb this kind of thing right now. Isn't there something we can do?'

'Indeed there is, my girl,' the other replied briskly. 'We shall go directly to the mansion where I shall simply demand that my husband do something.'

'Such as?'

'He is the governor, so he's supposed to know. Well, what are you waiting for, girl? For that ruckus to turn into some kind of shooting war?'

But there was no war. Not yet. By the time the women had secured a rig and circled around the crowded square, the sheriff and his deputies had intervened to quash the disturbance. But the seeds of violence had been sown and must surely germinate in the heat generated by the giant new technology of the railroad and the last-ditch battle waged against it by the Combine.

They found the governor calm enough as he organized his forces and issued orders in his quiet yet forceful way.

His wife appeared reassured by all this but Carrie's concerns had only deepened since their arrival. She had hoped to find Clay Rogan at the mansion. But nobody had sighted him since his very public clash with the gunman from Fort Such.

Everybody in the big smoke-filled upstairs supper-room of the Cattlemen's Club was showing visible signs of stress. All but 'the guest of honour', which was how he'd been introduced by Rade Tierney. Maybe Kip Silver was secretly impressed by this display of opulence and power, while the fawning flattery of three of the most powerful men in the county had been heady stuff indeed. But his good early feeling had not lasted. Now Osgood, Taylor and Quinn were destroying the good impression they'd created earlier as they wrangled and proposed and discarded propositions while puffing and coughing on fat cigars like there was no tomorrow.

The killer was directly responsible for the abrupt change of atmosphere that had come to these plush rooms. The cattle kings had instantly offered him a high-paying gun job right here in the city, and it was his counter-quote that had sent the big three into a spin.

Whenever the three glanced his way and remembered that bloated figure he had quoted, they found themselves reaching for their glasses again.

None of which bothered the guest of honour. Silver had been dealing with tightwads and 'men of destiny' all his life. They all screamed about financial ruin, but just about all caved in eventually.

He finally wearied of the wrangling and silenced the room by rising and picking up his hat.

'Five grand,' he said quietly. He flipped the hat and caught it. 'And remember, gentlemen, you were actually winning your war with the railroad before my old enemy from Fort Such showed. I'll give old Roge that. He's got enough front and bullshit to be able to turn a town on its ear if he wants, even one this size. But I'm telling you he can be taken and that I can do it. The way I see it, you will pay my asking price – or round about this time next week you'll be able to buy tickets for the run by rail from Capital City right up to the main line. So what's it to be?'

He was already heading for the big double doors as he spoke. Osgood appeared to be half-choking as he called him back. Tierney grinned in triumph as the killer hesitated for effect, then slowly turned and waited to hear what the still most powerful man in Capital City might have to say.

A giant circle. Rogan had been in it before. You strike out in a direction that appears promising, which offers hope, but when you get there you find you're back where you started. You've still got your gun and you know you'll have to use it or die. And this time, dying could be easier than ever before.

He slugged down a bitter mouthful of Midge Riddle's bite-back coffee and studied his image in the mirror. There was no way out, unless he chose to run. Run – and when at a safe distance, stand back and watch the best chance he'd ever had disappear down the drain.

Midge leaned ancient elbows on her counter top.

'You don't have to do it, Sonny Jim. Let him go shoot someone else. Who knows? Someone might get lucky and put him in the ground. Who says you've got to take him up just on account he's challenged you to gunfight? Man doesn't have to do anything he don't want to, does he?'

'I said it, lady,' he said bitterly. 'I swallowed his bait and now I can either choke on it or bring it up.'

'I ain't dead sure I understand what it is you're saying, son.'

'It's plain as paint,' he said roughly, rising from his bar stool. 'I'm saying I can either run and be branded coward the rest of my life . . . or I can face him and die! Some choice, huh?'

The half-filled joint fell silent at that. They knew he'd been drinking even if he did not appear drunk. He spoke clearly yet they were hard-put to understand the meaning of his words.

Rogan was far from drunk but also far from being his usual self. In a violent lifetime he had faced danger more times than he could rightly recall. Every time there had been a feeling deep inside that he would survive, and that feeling had never failed him.

But he'd never faced a Kip Silver before.

That was the cause of the feeling that gripped him tonight. He must do something to relieve his tensions. Now. Suddenly he strode from the room and went directly across to the livery where the old dark liveryman leaned against the door, looking hopefully for one last client before he slept.

Rogan spoke to the man. Money changed hands. Curious drinkers were emerging by the time Rogan reappeared. He was toting an old piece of two-by-four about six feet long. He laid the beam upon a ridge along the adobe wall of the livery some five feet off the ground. It sat there. Next he plucked a ten-dollar bill from his shirt pocket and handed it to a bewildered-looking liveryman.

'In case I miss and hit your wall, oldtimer . . . only I won't.'

He was even more sober than ever by now. But this was something he had to do. No good of a man just thinking he could win. He had to *know*. He had to know right now.

He stepped backwards several paces with every eye upon him. He stood motionless a moment, hand over Colt. Then he drew and heard the gasps of astonishment as hand and gun and screaming shell blurred into one single entity and, one after another, six tightly spaced black holes appeared in the piece of timber which trembled upon the ridge and finally fell to ground.

Somebody cheered, another cried 'Yeehahh!' But Rogan was already gone. He felt almost foolish, yet at the same time, triumphant. For in this longest of all nights the big man of the gun needed to know – not just believe – that the magic was still in his hand and eye. He knew he was never faster. Yet what he still could not be totally sure of, or submit to any test, would not be known until sometime after first light tomorrow when he went out to face down a man who was faster than anybody he had ever seen.

And wondered how many men over the years had faced him with that same uncertainty in *their* hearts.

CHAPTER 10

THE LAST DUEL

They were roistering at the Golden Spur. Everyone was making bets and talking big when the batwings banged open with a crash and the City Marshal came in and strode directly to the bar. He slapped hard with the flat of his hand.

'City Ordinance 105,' he snapped. 'All places selling liquor to close down by one. So drink up and get out.'

Scarcely a man moved. At first. Some had been prepared to drink all night then go out and grab the best lookout positions on the square at daybreak, where some experts reckoned they would see the gun duel of their lives. They'd figured that about the last man to have either the time or dedication to enforce the law book tonight would have to be Clay Rogan. Until that moment.

The bar man made to object but broke sharply off as Rogan swung on him.

'I'm walking across this room to the far side. If there's one customer left in this place by the time I get there, whoever it is will go straight to jail along with you, mister. So, now I'm walking.'

There was never an exodus like that at the Golden Spur before. As the last stumbling, foul-cussing reveller stumbled out through the batwings, the marshal was on his heels. He paused with hands upon the half doors for a final word for the hang-jawed man behind the bar.

'Five minutes and all lights out!' Then was gone, the swinging doors flapping to silence in his wake.

By the time Rogan reached the Glory Hole and Fancy Chett's, the word had already raced ahead of him, and was acted upon, for the word was that the marshal was in a mean mood. Soon bewildered drinkers and their ladies were grouped about in bewildered clusters upon the plaza square, when a familiar powerful figure suddenly reappeared from the far side and came striding towards them.

'Is he drunk?' someone whispered. Then he added, 'Well, I guess I would be too if I was planning to gunfight that cold-eyed young bastard out of Fort Such.'

'I dunno if he's drunk or sober,' another broke in, jumping down off a high porch to the ground and heading off. 'But I sure as hell don't mean to stay and find out.'

This scene was repeated a dozen times during the following hour, leaving evicted revellers and awak-ened citizens alike squinting anxiously around corners and from behind their windows in jittery expectation of whatever might happen next on this strangest of all nights. Just what had gotten into this rock of a man they had come to respect and admire over the past weeks? Rogan appeared neither drunk or crazy, but most reckoned he must be one or the other. Maybe both?

'Hey, lookit!' a bleary-eyed ex-patron of the Shining Angel whispered. 'He's finally stoppin' over yonder by the bank to light up. You reckon he's getting tired of shoving everyone about?'

'Well, looks everyone's finally shut down by this,' pointed out another. 'Maybe he's just ready to quit now.'

But the big man sporting the small silver badge did not quit then nor later. The moment he had his cheroot going to his satisfaction he set off for Poortown with his long driving stride, not once glancing back.

Nobody could recall the last time any trooper, peace officer or government official had been seen in Poortown after midnight. Down there along the river, the nights belonged to the poverty-stricken, the derelicts, the truly lost and the dangerous razor men, thugs and the last murderous losers of the city's once flourishing criminal class.

Until tonight, that was.

It took Rogan less than an hour to empty the streets of the sprawling slum, then dispatched three cuffed and bloodied troublemakers to the jailhouse with a jittery deputy driving the round-up wagon and him striding behind, six-gun in hand.

Next he headed for the railroad work site where

149

he ascertained that all was in order, and that the security measures imposed by the governor were being strictly observed.

The way he figured, should the worst kind of trouble overtake this city next day, he could at least guarantee he had all the potential added danger spots shut down or their denizens safely behind bars. He needed to have it that way. For although he'd imposed a powerful new brand of law upon a reluctant city over recent weeks, there was no guarantee it would remain that way – should something befall him.

For apart from the sheriff and maybe half a dozen others, nobody would willingly risk his life to maintain law and order should, say, the Combine and Kip Silver seize the reins of power in Capital City.

He was not being pessimistic, just realistic. He was encouraged by the fact that now, virtually every drunk, law-hater, troublemaker and son of a bitch in the city was off the streets and drying out, which would guarantee most would have to be stone cold sober and therefore represent no immediate danger come sunrise.

What might befall should he die in a storm of six-gun fire, was something he would be unable to control. But if that were the case, he'd die knowing he had done everything possible to stem that bloody tide.

Only then, with a bloated moon riding the night sky and the city below him quieter and more subdued at three in the morning than anyone had ever seen it before, did he finally relax and head slowly down the slope and make for the plaza.

He was satisfied that exactly every single action of his one-man clean-up campaign was strictly in keeping with the governor's own attitude towards law and order.

Fitzhenry had handed the pamphlet on that topic the day they made him a special city marshal. He realized the document was regarded as something of a joke by overworked Sheriff Tom Doherty and his deputies, and it was true he'd scarcely consulted the directive during his time here.

Until now.

Tonight was different from the moment Clay Rogan had suddenly realized he needed to experience what it was like to be – not just a man with a badge and a big gun to back it up – but a genuine dedicated officer of the law. To hold folks to the letter of the law and to deal ruthlessly yet fairly with anyone who defied it.

Just straight out, down-home, law enforcement made simple so everybody could understand it, and obey it.

As a result of his efforts he now felt better than he could have believed, and found himself pausing to gust cigar smoke into the air and gaze round at this uncommonly tranquil nightscape with a genuine feeling of belonging and achievement.

He'd needed to experience that at least once before. . . .

Before *what*, gunner? Go on, spit it out! Why tonight of all nights?

And that treacherous inner voice he'd been trying

to still all night seemed to whisper, 'You *do* reckon you're going to die . . . don't you, high-stepping Marshal Rogan?'

His hand dropped to gun handle when he heard the sudden clatter of hoofbeats from the alley by the general store.

A familiar buggy appeared and he blinked when he sighted Carrie Morelos seated alongside one of the governor's drivers upon the high seat.

What in hell. . . ?

The rig drew abreast and halted. The girl swung lithely down before the wheels had ceased turning. For a moment she just stood staring at him with a strange expression. Then she then rushed forward, throwing out her arms.

'Oh, you're all right. I thought . . . I mean I heard . . . I don't know what I thought.' Then calming, she held him at arm's length and fixed him with that familiar bossy look. 'Honestly, Clay Rogan, just what do you think you are doing? I just couldn't believe my ears when I was told you were responding to some gun criminal's stupid challenge by rushing about in the middle of the night acting as though you'd lost your senses.'

She paused to gesture.

'So I came down to see for myself, and what do I find? A ghost town! Just what on earth do you think you are doing? And, more importantly, why?'

He stared at her blankly. She considered herself highly sophisticated and knowledgeable, he knew. Likely she was. But she could have no notion about such harsh realities as 'The Code', under which men like himself – and yes, a killer such as Kip Silver – lived and often died by. It was a primitive and uniquely Western code of the gunfighter, he would allow. Yet a man could not break it without being branded a coward. Maybe all that would change in time, but maybe not in his lifetime.

Reacting to his silence she reached up and squeezed his shoulders, expression softening again.

'This is not you. Why? Can't you at least tell me why you are prepared to risk your life this way? Surely you're not obliged to respond? The governor could simply authorize that Fort Such butcher's arrest and knock this childish foolishness on the head in a moment. But only if you agreed to withdraw and—'

'Sorry, I can't do that, Carrie,' he cut in grimly. 'But your coming here means one hell of a lot to me. I hope to get to tell you just how much . . . later. . . .'

Her eyes filled with tears as she dropped her hands. 'He'll kill you. I can see it in your eyes. He'll kill you, this stupid town won't care, and you'll be gone and I . . . I'll be on my own!'

He was dazed by her words, exhilarated. Yet words would not come. He raised his hand impotently – a long moment's taut silence – and then she was turning and rushing away.

The tension drained from him leaving him weak. He groaned then signalled to the driver who jumped down to help Carrie up into the rig, then clambered up beside her, clucked to the horses, and swiftly drove off.

Clay turned away like an old man.

Looking up, he saw that virtually every window

upon the square showed at least one pale, staring face.

Would sunrise never come?

Rogan sat fully-clothed in the darkness of the jail-house cell where he had spent the past hour, not asleep, just smoking and watching the night move silently by the high barred window.

Then came the faintest hint of grey and he knew the longest night of his life was drawing to an end.

His life with it?

That was the Ghost of Dead Gunfighters whispering in his ear, he realized. He forced a grin, teeth locked together and appearing starkly white against his bronzed skin in this jailhouse dawn. He flexed his shoulders, acutely conscious in that moment of the great power of his body, the subtle awareness of all those veins, capillaries, bones, muscles, tissues and brain cells functioning so perfectly . . . like he was Immortality Man.

Never before a gunfight in the past had he been troubled by the faintest doubt. Until now. So, he reasoned, if everything was different this time, he should forget about keeping himself solitary and aloof and react differently also. Be with people. Look up friends. Share the tension and maybe draw strength from others – the way a normal man might.

With an effort he sought to bring those friends up on his memory file. Yet found he could think of but one name, saw only the single face.

Carrie Morelos.

He stood up and grimaced. There was irony for

you! It seemed the lonely man of the gun had unwittingly met the one woman who might change his life, yet had done so at almost the exact same time and place that saw him committed to a duel that might prove to be his last.

Tough luck, eh, gunner?

The toughest, or so it might seem.

Only time and daybreak would tell.

Capital City had pretended to sleep but nobody was deceived. A few might have dozed a little, yet the vast majority had found themselves totally incapable of even lying down, much less closing their eyes. So the many eyes of the city seemed red-rimmed and glassy as they found themselves suddenly and silently alerted by the ghostliest streak of light limning the eastern skyline above the desert.

Soon the full roaring day would be on the march!

Yet it was still dark between the clapboards, the fanged roofs of the hotels, business emporiums and in the carefully tended gardens of the governor's mansion. In mere moments it seemed ghostly figures materialized in grey silence to be glimpsed eventiually creeping, crawling or jostling their half-sighted way through the deep gloom of streets, lanes and alleyways, all with the same destination.

The great Square of the Heroes.

Long before the first strong rays streaked across that somnolent sky the sharpsters and trades folk, the flim-flam men, found prime viewing positions upon verandahs, stoops and even rooftops. When the initial rush of full daylight finally arrived it immediately lifted from the gloom the hundreds of faces, pale faces, expectant faces, the faces of rich and poor, the young, old, sick and diseased – all of them briefly if powerfully united by something which many did not really want to see, yet could not resist. The drama of death played out before their very eyes.

It was barbaric.

It was the West.

Soon there came the loud creaking of wheels, the squeaking of unoiled axles. It was the sound of the wagons bringing the railroad workers down from their track-end, still a half-mile from completion beyond the fast-rising depot building.

Then came the water wagon, driven by an Indian and laden down by visiting firemen and sightseers from outside the city, rumbling noisily across the river bridge with polished harness glittering, the passengers growing as excited as if on their way to the county fair as they caught the first glimpse of an already half- filled square.

Rogan came like a night-walker along the ill-fitted plankwalk boards. He did not hesitate upon reaching the square, did not even slow when a ragged cheer went up, and someone bawled lustily: 'See, I told you he wouldn't show yeller. What price you got him set at now, Lucky?'

Someone laughed but most were quieter now and deathly serious as they watched the big figure shoulder the throng and move out to the centre of the square by the well, walking neither fast or slowly.

Alone, so starkly alone.

The sun by now had broken free of the Sundance

Hills hills to flood the Square of the Heroes arena with golden light. It winked warmly from the copper pots hanging from the front porch of the hardware store . . . and somewhere a woman sobbed as if only now realizing it was all too real, not some entertaining fantasy staged for their enjoyment, as she might have imagined.

And suddenly Kip Silver was also out there in the open space, as eye-catching and finely turned out as a young man calling upon a girl for their very first date.

A thousand eyes hungrily devoured the pageantry and drama of it all, and they hushed expectantly now as Silver moved leisurely towards the square centre while Rogan remained where he was standing by the well.

Then both men turned and faced.

No brag, no carefully rehearsed final words. These men were pros, and few were ever more experienced in, nor more acutely conscious of, all the crimson historical ritual invoked in this drama of life and death they were about to perform.

One would live and one die. That was the black-and-white reality of every duel to the death.

And it was only in that final hushed moment that Rogan finally found himself able to acknowledge that truth which he had been denying ever since the kid rode into town.

He did not believe he could win.

There it was – out at last!

For he had seen Kip Silver in a gunfight, and ever since that day had considered the younger man to be the fastest of the fast, the nonpareil of the Colts. He had never conceded that terrible truth even in his private thoughts – until this moment of truth, and now would never be given the opportunity to do so.

Well, so be it.

The die was cast and the time for confessions, fears or delusions of superiority was long gone.

All there was left was the moment, and the gladiators did not let down their vast audience.

Each man stood straight and motionless as they faced across fifty yards of cobblestones, hands hanging loose and ready at their sides. No taunting last words, no hint of fear in either face. Just the grim ritual of death both had believed in and lived by, about to be acted one more time.

There was no signal.

Suddenly it was simply the time. As one, two hands swept down in blurring motion too swift for the eye to follow, and Clay's big Peacemaker was still whipping up when his adversary's weapon reached firing level and filled the great silence with its defiant bellow.

Instant pain seared Rogan's left shoulder and he felt the blood gush hotly.

He was proven right. Silver *was* the faster!

Yet in that same immeasurable fragment of time, one lightning-bolt thought was followed by the other.

Silver had cleared and triggered – *too* fast!

As if in slowed-down motion, Clay saw through the gunsmoke that smoking gunbarrel making the slight correction necessary to set the foresight upon his heart. But by this Clay's big iron was levelled and locked in on its living target in his fist. Calm as a hanging judge in Heaven, and focused as never before in that one crimson speck of time . . . Rogan was stroking Colt trigger.

The bellow of his Colt sounded like the crack of doom. Instantly his adversary was flung backwards with his weapon spinning high and unfired from his grip. Silver swayed from side to side with both empty hands attempting to reach his exploded forehead where dark blood gushed hotly. Then his four limbs went limp and he fell full length in the deep dust and never moved again.

Slowly lowering his weapon, Clay saw how small the man now appeared, with knees drawn up to his chest and frozen hands covering his face as though his last thought had been to hide from the world the fact that Kip Silver was dead.

By the time Clay Rogan was strong enough to appear on the streets again, it was all but over. Judge Michael Moran from Ranger Headquarters, whose nick-name was Blood and Thunder Moran, had lived up to his sobriquet by the manner in which he'd piece-by-piece uncovered the entire ugly tapestry of the Combine's felonies over the years, and promptly consigned all three to the territorial prison for terms ranging from ten to twenty years.

The railroad was completed during his convales-cence and would shortly haul its first cargo of prime local beef back to Larribee none of which news drew even a comment from Rogan that day.

He had far more important matters to consider on

a fine fall morning when he presented himself at the governor's mansion to receive his official promotion as permanent City Marshal of Capital City.

Reunited finally with his wife during Rogan's spell at the Centre the governor waxed verbose and perhaps overly-complimentarily during the brief ceremony, and was somewhat taken back when this new appointee suddenly interrupted his words, adjusted his shoulder sling, and excused himself.

Only Isabel Fitzhenry understood that the man whom she considered had virtually saved their city was eager to come to grips with the *real* goal and challenge of his life that day, namely persuading someone beautiful to marry him.

Isobel Fitzhenry was assured his proposal would be accepted. She felt that if she and the governor believed they might succeed again, as both did at that moment, then the high-bred daughter of Juan Carlos Morelos and the former gunner from Fort Such should find it as easy as, say, pinning on a new brass star and taking over as the governor's right-hand man and designated lieutenant.

Anything and everything seemed possible in that peaceful leaf-fall season in Capital City.